JUST SIGN HERE

CARA DEE

Just Sign Here

Copyright © 2020 by Cara Dee
All rights reserved

Edited by Silently Correcting Your Grammar, LLC.
Formatted by Eliza Rae Services.

WELCOME TO CAMASSIA COVE

Camassia Cove is a town in northern Washington created to be the home of some exciting love stories. Each novel taking place here is a standalone—with the exception of sequels and series within the CC universe—and they vary in genre and pairing. What they all have in common is the town in which they live. Some are friends and family. Others are complete strangers. Some have vastly different backgrounds. Some grew up together. It's a small world, and many characters will cross over and pay a visit or two in several books—Cara's way of giving readers a glimpse into the future of their favorite characters. Oh, who is she kidding; they are characters she's unable of saying good-bye to. But, again, each novel stands on its own, and spoilers will be avoided as much as possible.

If you're interested in keeping up with secondary characters, the town, the timeline, and future novels, check out Camassia Cove's own website at www.camassiacove.com. There you will also see which characters have gotten their own books already, where they appear, which books are in the works, character profiles, and you'll be treated to a taste of the town.

*

Get social with Cara
www.caradeewrites.com
www.camassiacove.com
Facebook: @caradeewrites
Twitter: @caradeewrites
Instagram: @caradeewrites

DEDICATION

This book goes out to every year except for 2020.

2020, you suck.

Go stand in the corner and
think about what you've done.

CHAPTER I.

In retrospect, it's easy to see which event changed my life forever. The day you walked into my work, handsome as all hell—no, seriously, the motherfucking epitome of silver fox, in a three-piece suit, no less—and you said you were looking for me.

Me.

But the first time I really felt the shift, like something momentous was happening, something I wouldn't be able to walk away from unscathed, was when you gave me three little words.

"Just sign here."

"Daddy!" Julia shrieked.

I ignored her and placed her luggage by the elevator, then stalked into the kitchen to grab her sippy cup and snack pack. I was in desperate need of a shower, but a look at the clock told me I'd lost my opportunity around the time I was cleaning oatmeal and applesauce off the floor. After which, Julia had promptly thrown her sticky spoon right in my face.

"You dumb!" she yelled at me.

1

I gritted my teeth and drew a deep breath. We had a flight to catch; Cathryn would be here any minute, thank *God*. She could deal with my little terror's tantrum.

Whoever said that toddlers were adorable had never met mine. Something had happened when she turned two—almost overnight. It felt like she hadn't stopped screaming since. Four months until she turned three; we'd find out if I lived to see the day.

She let out a wail and started tugging off her clothes in the living room, and I stopped with my luggage in hand and merely stared at her. There was always something wrong. Her dress, her hair, her shoes, how her bed was made, the scent of her shampoo, whatever she ate, and, once, how her teddy bear had *looked* at her.

Truth be told, I missed her. She'd been there for me, whether she'd wanted to or not, while I grieved the loss of her mothers. She'd been a sweet baby. Quiet. She'd slept through the night from an early age. In short, she'd made my first year of fatherhood very easy. Until her second birthday. My penthouse had become a war zone. Vases had crashed to the ground, same with picture frames, and there wasn't a single piece of furniture she wouldn't use her crayons and markers on. If she gave me a hug that lasted more than a second, I considered myself lucky.

"Are you finished?" I asked impatiently.

There she stood, a naked little ball of fury, fire shooting out of her blue eyes, her face red, and her dark hair pointing in every direction.

The sight of her made my heart clench. To think, I was only supposed to be her godfather.

"I don't wanna fly," Julia snarled.

I suppressed a sigh and grabbed the tie I'd left in the hall. "You love flying, darling."

"Not now!" she screamed.

Thankfully, the elevator dinged, and Cathryn appeared as my daily savior.

"Tell me you have more resumés for me to read through on the plane," I said. "If I don't find a good nanny soon, I... It doesn't matter what I do."

She smiled in sympathy and tucked a piece of her blond hair behind her ear, and her heels clicked on the floor on her way into the living room. "That bad, huh? Oh my. Good morning, Julia. Let's get you dressed, shall we?" She turned back to me. "You go wait in the car."

"Thank you." I didn't waste a second. I loaded the luggage into the elevator and headed down.

I blew out a breath and rubbed my temples. Right, my tie. I faced the mirrored wall and tied it.

I had a nanny for Julia, technically. But Cathryn had her own family and couldn't take care of my daughter past work hours. And to make matters worse, my PA quit last week. She'd told me she was going back to school—in May?—but the gossip at the office said otherwise. She'd found me too *bossy*.

I'd been her boss, goddammit!

If she only knew how much I held back these days. Once upon a time, control had been everything to me. I still craved it every damn day, but I wasn't likely to get a taste of it again anytime soon.

Soon-to-be three-year-olds didn't obey as well as submissive adults.

I nodded in greeting to Paul, who opened the door for me.

"Good morning, Mr. Delamare. Your car is here."

"Thank you, Paul." I aimed straight for Mathis as he popped the trunk. He was responsible for all my transportation, including air travel, and I was happy to have him with me. He was the only one who'd been with me for longer than five years. More than that, he was the only one who didn't have a higher position in his sights. He was perhaps a year or two younger than me, and he'd reached his goals. He got to travel as a work perk, which gave him the opportunity to see the world and catch up with friends from his past in the Army. "Good morning, Mathis."

"Morning, boss." He took care of the luggage while I got in the car and pulled out my phone.

I was still unfamiliar with keeping track of my own schedule, but I'd have a six-hour flight to sort through all the meetings I had this week. Hopefully, our West Coast people would shed some light on the problems we were facing here in Boston and at our other East Coast locations.

Four years in a row, our hotels out here had received slightly worse ratings than the previous year. We didn't know why, although I had my suspicions, and I had sent several teams to figure out the issues—to no avail. This time, I was going myself, starting with the West Coast, where Westwater remained a popular choice for business travelers and continuously received good ratings.

A moment later, a scream filled the car as Cathryn arrived with Julia.

"She says she's hungry," Cathryn told me.

"Perhaps she shouldn't have thrown her breakfast on the floor," I muttered, sending a quick email before pocketing my phone. I sighed and watched Julia struggle against Cathryn, who buckled her into her booster seat. "She wanted toast for breakfast, so I made her that. Then she changed her mind and wanted oatmeal." Mainly because she loved applesauce, which I put in her oatmeal. "That resulted in a tantrum," I went on. "In the end, she ate a yogurt cup while I mopped the floor."

"Sounds to me like you're testing your father's limits, sweetie." Cathryn touched Julia's cheek, wiping away her tears.

4

I lifted a brow. "Testing them? She's driving a pink bulldozer all over them."

Cathryn let out a laugh.

"Let's call these three for interviews when we get back to Boston." I placed the three resumés on the hallway table in our hotel suite for Cathryn. "They're the best of the worst."

"Good grief," Cathryn decreed. "Remind me why I let you recruit me to be a traveling babysitter?"

"I believe a substantial raise played a part," I replied, adjusting my tie, and she nodded and tapped her nose. I mustered a smirk. "I'll see you tonight."

Soon, I was back in the car downstairs, and I felt marginally refreshed after my shower.

It was the second year Cathryn had played nanny for Julia when I was on the road, and with a bit of luck, I'd steal her away next year too. Back home, things were different. She worked part time in HR with the company and only a couple hours a day for me personally.

I sat back in the town car and glimpsed the last of the Seattle lunch rush outside the window.

Wanting to relax for a moment before my first meeting, I asked Mathis to turn on the radio. It would help keep my work-related headache at bay.

"...and with us today, we have our own Peyton Scott, a hotel manager here in Seattle. Welcome to *MommyTalk*, Peyton."

I snorted under my breath. Perhaps a radio talk show about parenting could tell me what I was doing wrong. And why I didn't have the same stories to share as all the parents online. I may have stayed up several nights, scouring the internet for help. All I got were these sickeningly sweet tales of how amazing their children were, how adorable they were as they developed, and how funny they were when they got into trouble.

I wasn't laughing.

A masculine voice replied, letting me know Peyton probably wasn't a mommy. "Thank you. It feels good to be on a show that isn't constantly on the verge of being shut down due to declining listeners."

The female host laughed. "That's right, Peyton is part of the WX family and hosts his own show here on Channel 8 called *Throwback,* and it airs every Thursday at ten PM," she said. "If you like history, make sure to tune in." She paused. "So, as mentioned before, Father's Day is coming up in a couple weeks, and that's why we're switching it up a little throughout May. Instead of listening to us mommies, we want to give the floor to all the wonderful daddies out there. In this case, it's a brother. You single-handedly raised your younger sister, Peyton. You were only nineteen when you got custody. That must've been difficult but rewarding."

"Still waiting for the reward," Peyton joked. My mouth twitched. "But yeah, for a few years. Anna was a year old when I started taking care of her, and I was all she had until she turned seven."

"That's amazing," the woman gushed. "How old is Anna now?"

"She's fifteen."

That made Peyton thirty-three. I couldn't help but wonder where the mother and fath—

"Boss, would you like me to change—"

"Shh! No. Thank you." My pulse spiked at my own outburst, and I had to take a breath. Christ.

It was just a radio show. No reason to get dramatic.

"...but to be honest, it was freaking hard," Peyton was saying.

"I was understandably clueless about children, and Anna was a demon. I don't think I went to work a single time those first two or three years without a food stain on my clothes. Most days, I was fumbling in the dark and just doing my best. There were a lot of downs before I had any ups."

I enjoyed his voice—and what he was saying. Honesty about the hardships of parenthood was always refreshing in a world where everything had to look perfect on social media.

If I saw one more mother with a blinding Colgate smile after spending the day with her four kids *and* making cinnamon rolls, I was going to call my lawyers and sue someone, because it had to be bullshit.

The radio host chuckled, a sound that didn't sound entirely genuine. "It's true. We do struggle at times—of course—but after a little bit of rain comes so much sunshine."

I let out a hmpf.

"Sometimes," Peyton replied uncertainly. "Thing is, I don't understand why we have to glorify raising children. I love my sister beyond words, and we will always be close, but she was by no means easy to take care of. Are children supposed to be? I don't believe so. What I believe parenthood consists of—at least when the children are young—are sleepless nights, stained clothes, chaos, and occasional headaches. And this doesn't mean it's not worth it—the opposite. We love our kids to the point where it's worth all those sleepless nights and all the anxiety."

I smiled.

"A toddler smiling and sitting pretty in the cart at the grocery store isn't proof of good parenting," Peyton went on. "Same with all the blogs and social media accounts where we get bombarded with pictures of perfection." Christ. Had he read my mind? "It's wonderful that we get those memories too, but it's become a contest to show who's happiest. Who's succeeding the most. Meanwhile, the tough moments are hidden away and

7

suppressed. We don't talk about it, because we're afraid of being judged."

I released a breath, unable to describe the emotions that surged forward. But he was saying everything I needed to hear.

"Parenthood isn't picture-perfect," Peyton said, "and I don't want it to be. I'd rather look at my sister now and see the head-strong girl I raised. I can think back on the times I tried to make cookies with her, and we ended up with a flour explosion in the kitchen—not to mention some slammed doors because she was furious when the cookies looked like something that'd been eaten and thrown up."

I laughed softly.

"But she's a perfectionist today," Peyton added with a smile in his voice. "She's ambitious and creative, and she's learned from several years of mistakes and projects gone wrong. She's learned to control her temper a bit too—thankfully—because she's experienced how quickly she can mess things up by blowing her fuse."

That was the type of person I wanted to help me with Julia.

"I'm not saying we should hide the progress our children make. I'm just saying we shouldn't be afraid to showcase the struggles," Peyton summed up. "Today it's even worse, too. Ten years ago, I could at least go online without thinking that everyone was perfect and I was the screw-up who failed to take care of my sister."

There it was. I'd thought similar things before, especially after searching for help online. It could be alienating to read all the success stories.

Peyton worked as a hotel manager, didn't he? I remembered the host saying something about that in the beginning of the show.

"Boss, we're here," Mathis told me.

"A moment." I pulled out my phone and texted my cousin back in Boston.

I need a favor. Can you have your assistant find a Peyton Scott for me? He works as a hotel manager, presumably in Seattle. 33 years old.

CHAPTER
2.

I was down to my last forty-eight hours in Seattle when I learned about Peyton's workplace. And he wasn't the manager. He was the front office manager. The radio show host must've gotten it wrong, but either way, it made it easier for me to approach Peyton if he was actually at the hotel as opposed to being holed up in an office somewhere.

Ironically, he worked at a hotel we'd once made a bid for. In the end, Hilton had offered more money and given it a much-needed makeover, and I entered the lavish lobby a little past noon.

I wouldn't have chosen gold and blue for the theme, not with those marble pillars there, but it wasn't my hotel. In my opinion, you could choose marble or gold, never both. Classy and elegant could quickly take a turn for gaudy.

Four men and women staffed the long check-in counter, and I cocked my head at a fifth who appeared from an office in the back. His suit was tailored to fit his body; it was more than just a uniform. He smiled crookedly at something one of the women said, then nodded and proceeded to touch base with the others.

It had to be Peyton, in which case... Fucking hell, he was a beautiful young man. Striking, truly. Green eyes, hair darker than my own, but untidier, a lovely swimmer's body... I wondered what he'd look like on his knees, peering up at me with those gorgeous eyes and my come staining his lips.

I cleared my throat and curbed the image. Those urges had no place in my life anymore.

I did hope he was single, though. Working for me would take him away from Seattle for long periods of time, and a wife or girlfriend could easily get in the way of any amount of money I offered him.

Even his posture was perfect. He smiled politely as I approached, and he kept his hands clasped behind his back.

"Welcome to the International, sir," the young woman next to Peyton greeted. "Do you have an early check-in?"

I slid her a quick, courteous smile before returning my attention to Peyton. "I believe it's you I'm looking for. Are you Peyton Scott?"

His brows lifted a fraction, curiosity evident in his expression. "I am. How may I assist you?"

Don't ask that question.

"It's a private matter," I replied.

"Ah." He gestured toward the nearest seating area. "I will be right with you, sir. May I offer you coffee or tea?"

"Coffee, thank you." On the way over to a set of plush couches, I adjusted my tie and cuff links, ready to use my charm if I had to. One way or another, I wanted to recruit him. Perhaps he would make a terrific assistant, given his job here. But first and foremost, I wanted to see how he would interact with my daughter.

He joined me shortly after and took a seat across from me after setting a cup of coffee on the table for me.

The problem with hotel lobbies—they were too big for private conversations, and the furniture was positioned too far apart.

"I heard you on the radio the other day." I leaned forward

and took a sip of the coffee. Too bland. "Not your history show," I clarified. "You spoke about parenting."

"Oh." He shifted in his seat, unsure of where I was going with this. Perhaps wondering how I'd found him. "Was there a problem, sir?"

"On the contrary," I said. "I work in the hotel business myself, and I wanted to discuss the possibility of recruiting you."

His forehead creased, and he tilted his head. "Based on a radio show about parenthood?"

I flashed him a smile. "I have a daughter and could relate to everything you said. It made me want to meet with you. What your position would be with me depends on you. I need a personal assistant, and I need help with my daughter." I cleared my throat and gave him the shortest explanation possible. "Right now, I have a nanny who travels with me. It's a temporary solution. However, if I were to find an assistant with as great parenting skills as you seem to have, one who could develop a good relationship with the nanny too—"

"I apologize for interrupting, sir, but I fear you might've made a mistake," he said uncertainly. "I'm not what most would qualify as a good parent, and I know for certain that I won't be invited back to that show. Sharon was livid with me afterward."

If anything, it made my desire to hire him grow tenfold. "I'm not looking for what's already out there. I've spent weeks discarding resumés from nannies who aren't half as honest as you are. And I suppose that's what it boils down to. The honesty. I want to be able to see my daughter at the end of the day and know she's been in the hands of someone who sees raising her for what it is. The dirtiest job on the planet."

Peyton's mouth twisted up slightly. "Is she that bad?"

"At the moment? She's worse."

"How old is she?"

"She'll be three in September. Nothing works. She can love something for five seconds and then declare it's the worst thing in the world. Her tantrums—I won't go there. But I feel as if I've tried everything at this point. From disciplining her to ignoring her when she starts screaming, from rewarding good behavior to distracting her from whatever's making her mad."

Peyton let out a low whistle.

"Does this mean you're alone with her?"

"Yes." I wasn't going into why. We didn't know each other well enough for that.

"So, let me get this straight," he said, facing me full on. "You're looking for a PA who will be with you by day, all while maintaining a close relationship with the other nanny, and then by night, the PA dons the nanny cap. You want someone to stay with you literally twenty-four seven. Who would agree to that?"

"Someone young and driven," I responded. "Someone who wouldn't mind putting their own life on hold for a year or two while securing their future financially."

He narrowed his eyes at me. A fucking adorable sight. "Who *are* you?"

Ah. Perhaps I should've introduced myself sooner. No matter. I reached forward and extended a hand. "Edward Delamare. Reluctant heir of Westwater Hotels."

"I guess you could afford it," he muttered, shaking my hand. He had long, slender fingers. God, I wanted them in places. "Why reluctant?"

I shrugged and sat back again. "That's a story for another day, but we all have our responsibilities. I admired my grandfather a great deal, and when he asked me personally to take a more hands-on position with the company before he passed, I couldn't refuse."

There were only two heirs left today. My cousin and me.

I could tell that Peyton didn't know how to respond, or

where we'd go from here, so I continued. "I have two days left in the city. Should you call in sick tomorrow and shadow me for twenty-four hours, I'd make sure you'd be compensated generously. You'd meet Julia, my daughter, and Cathryn, her nanny."

"What about your current PA?"

"I don't have one. She quit last week."

"Oh." He pinched his bottom lip and glanced toward the check-in counter, then back at me. "How often do you travel?"

"Usually only a month or two out of the year, in total, but this year is hectic," I admitted. "I'm on the road most of the time. Cathryn has graciously agreed to accompany me on all trips throughout the summer, but then she's going to stay home more. She has a family of her own to be there for." And two well-behaved kids in high school.

Peyton furrowed his brow. "Shouldn't Julia be at day care or something?"

I inclined my head. "Right now, I'm traveling too much, and I want her with me. But when I'm in Boston, she's at the company's day care from seven to five." The problem was that I usually worked from seven to seven. That was when Cathryn helped me, outside of her own position in HR, which I explained to Peyton.

"Got it." He was thinking about it, at least. He stretched out the seconds that passed, and his knee bounced.

I took another sip of my coffee. "Where does your sister live now?"

He looked at me like it was the strangest question. "At home with our mom."

"Ah, I thought you said—"

"That's a story for another day," he mimicked.

My mouth twitched, and I couldn't help myself. "Don't get smart with me."

Amusement danced in his eyes.

Tempting boy, this one.

"Do you enjoy traveling?" I wondered. He needed to hear some of the perks he'd get for working alongside me.

"I wouldn't know," he replied. "I haven't gotten the chance yet—except for last year. I went to LA to help a friend, but that's as far as I've been."

Interesting. He was used to being there for others. He'd raised his sister, and he'd worked hard; he had to.

"In the next few weeks, I'll be traveling up and down the West Coast," I revealed. "Then I'll have a month touring our locations in the Caribbean before I go to Chicago, Houston, Denver, and Las Vegas. With stops home in Boston here and there."

We had more locations across the country, but I'd hand-picked a selection in our most popular destinations.

"Jeesh." Peyton's eyebrows raised farther. "So, my job would be to babysit you during the day and babysit Julia at night."

Oh, how I wanted to toy with him for that. Fuck it, I wanted to prey on him. He was a brat. A feisty little brat.

This was excellent, though. He'd moved on from "Your PA would" to "I would."

He was carefully picturing himself in the position.

I was not-so-carefully picturing him in another position.

He'd certainly make my showers more interesting if he worked for me. Perhaps it *was* best if he had a wife or girlfriend who waited for him at home. I was going to need some firmly set boundaries in order to keep my promise. That time of my life was over and done with. I had Julia now.

"I mean, I would be there too," I told him, clearing my throat. "I'm not a distant father, by any means. Just clueless. I need help, definitely, but I was raised by nannies. I don't want that for her."

More than that, I didn't want it for myself. I spent a week

away from Julia last year and thought I was going to have a heart attack.

"You're serious about this," Peyton stated. "You haven't even seen my resumé."

"I'm serious about giving you a trial run," I replied. "I've heard enough to know that much. If you could extend the twenty-four hours to a week, even better. And you're welcome to call my office in Boston. Or hell, look into me online. Whatever you need."

He ran a hand through his hair and exhaled a small laugh. "I just got this position a few months ago. My first job where I don't have to worry about making rent."

"Working for me would be your second, then," I said. "How much do you make here? Around forty-five? You could make five or six times that with me—and you wouldn't have any rent to pay. You'd live with me, of course."

A thought that was more appealing than it should be.

"Jesus Christ," Peyton chuckled, scrubbing his hands over his face. "Well, um. I'd be stupid not to do the trial run, at least. Fuck it, right? We only live once. But I'll still look into you online."

Thank fuck.

I smiled. "Terrific. We'll meet up for breakfast at my hotel tomorrow. I'm staying at our Pier 62 location, and I'll make sure the staff knows you're expected." I nodded at his suit. "Consider that your dress code."

"I'm not saying it was wrong, Edward," Cathryn amended. "Just...bold. He could be anyone."

"So can any guy with a resumé," I pointed out.

"Well, that guy of yours is late now."

I checked my watch. "He'll be here." I hoped.

Julia came running out from our bedroom with a scowl. "I'm hungwy."

I pointed toward the dining area past the living room. "Room service was just delivered. Any chance I can get a hug this morning?"

"No!" She stalked between the two sofas and almost stumbled on the carpet. "Daddy, help meeee! Wait. No."

I scratched my forehead and exchanged a look with Cathryn.

"Do you think something is wrong with her?" I felt bad for asking, but I couldn't help but wonder.

"No, sir." Cathryn's gaze softened. "I think she's just—"

Two firm knocks on the door cut our topic short, and I headed for the entryway.

It was a visibly winded Peyton, who was, if possible, even more gorgeous with his cheeks flushed.

"Sorry I'm late," he said, taking a breath. "I assumed we'd have breakfast in the restaurant."

Ah. My fault for not having been clearer. "I should've been more specific. I apologize. Please come in, Peyton." I opened the door wider and dropped my gaze while he trailed toward Cathryn. Goddamn. What an exquisite, tight, round little ass.

It'd been much too long since I'd gotten laid.

Peyton and Cathryn handled their introductions on their own, and then I swooped in to take him to Julia.

"Darling, come meet a new friend." I found her on the other side of the dining table, trying to reach for the bowl of blueberries. "This is Peyton. He's going to spend some time with us."

She became shy in a heartbeat, though I knew it wouldn't last very long. She wasn't a shy girl. That said, I wasn't complaining that it drove her into my embrace at the moment. She darted for me and lifted her arms.

"Hi, Julia." Peyton smiled at her as I picked her up and positioned her on my hip. "That's a cool dress."

Julia shook her head and buried her face against my neck. "S'not cool, Daddy. Tell him."

I sent Peyton an apologetic look before I took my seat at the head of the table. "He thinks it's cool, and so do I." I squeezed her to me, taking every chance I got, and kissed her hair. "What would you like to eat, darling?"

"But, *ohhhh*," she whined and pushed me away. Then she scrambled off my lap and ran through the living room and into our bedroom again. I blew out a breath and fanned out a napkin across my lap. Fuck, it bothered me. It *hurt*. There was pressure on my chest, and I had to swallow hard. There had to be something I was doing wrong.

"So, that's Julia." I cleared my throat. My mood had soured instantly, and I avoided eye contact while I poured my coffee.

"I'll go talk to her," Cathryn started.

"Actually—may I?" Peyton asked. "If I'm going to be spending time with her, she might as well get to know me a bit."

Cathryn hesitated and glanced at me for a final answer.

"Have at it," I said tiredly. "She's likely to scream until you go deaf."

Peyton smirked wryly. "I'm immune. Just...let me have a go. Don't barge in if she does start yelling. I'll leave the door open, but—"

"We'll wait here," I assured. Then added, "We'll just listen in, I should say. We won't interrupt."

He nodded in acknowledgment before making his way toward the bedroom.

I sipped my coffee and debated whether to go stand by the door right away or if I should give him a couple minutes. But I had to eat if I was going to last through four meetings before lunch.

"What is it about him?" Cathryn asked me. "If I interpreted you correctly, he doesn't have any experience outside his own family. He's not a professional."

"Neither am I." I grabbed a triangle of toast and opened a butter pat. "I'm not looking for the perfect way or a smothering Englishwoman who puts more effort into cleaning up your language than making sure you're feeling all right." That about summed up my own childhood. "Peyton is real. He's young. He's not afraid to get his hands dirty."

Cathryn lost some tension in her shoulders and nodded once. "Okay. You know I'm on your side, sir."

That was when Julia began screaming.

I was out of my seat at the same time as my heart jumped up in my throat, and we both made our way through the living room.

"Why are you screaming?" I heard Peyton ask. "Should I start too?"

Cathryn and I came to a screeching halt before we reached the doorway, but I wasn't quite satisfied. I had to see, if only a little. I inched closer and closer until I saw Julia standing up in the middle of my bed, screaming at the top of her lungs, while Peyton leaned casually against one of the closet doors. He couldn't see me from his angle, meaning I wasn't going anywhere.

I watched him approach her slowly, hands in his pockets.

"Nooo!" she shrieked.

"If you don't tell me why you're upset, I will get upset too," he told her. "It's your choice, Julia."

He wasn't kidding. When Julia wouldn't stop screaming, Peyton stunned me by joining in once he was close enough to her. He yelled outright, causing Julia to scream even louder. But Peyton wouldn't be bested, evidently. He cranked it up until Julia collapsed on the bed with tears streaming down her face.

"Go'way!" she wailed.

"No." Peyton calmly sat down on the edge of the bed and stroked her back carefully. "That's the thing about me. I don't go away. It doesn't matter how much you scream or how much you cry. I'll be here to figure out what's wrong."

Julia hiccuped around a sob. "Don't yell more."

"It's not fun, is it?" Peyton murmured. "It can even be scary, right?"

She sniffled and nodded, and I recognized the signs in her. She was getting tired. It was like this every time she got upset. She screamed herself exhausted.

"Okay. I won't yell again," he promised. "Can we be friends?"

"I dunno," she whimpered.

"Do you have many friends at home?" he wondered.

She held up two fingers and wiped her nose on her arm.

"That's nice." Peyton smiled. "Do you play together?"

"Yeah. Wiv dolls and in a sambox."

"I loved playing in the sandbox when I was little," Peyton replied. "And do you know the best thing about being friends?" When she shook her head, he said, "When something is wrong, you can whisper it to your friend so they know. Then they can help you make things right again."

I felt my heart rate slow down again, and I let out a breath.

"I dunno," she sniffled, getting upset once more, though not as much.

"You don't know why you're sad?" Peyton asked.

"No," she cried.

"But that's a good answer, sweetheart." Peyton stroked her back soothingly. And while my immediate worry had lessened, another replaced it. I'd been down this road with her before. She wasn't completely impossible to communicate with; she even had moments where she was utterly adorable. But if she genuinely didn't know where this rage came from, how would I be able to help? How could I make it better?

I despised feeling helpless.

"You don't have to know why you're upset," Peyton went on in a comforting tone. "When it happens, you can try to tell us. Tell us that you're starting to get sad or angry but don't know why, and we will come up with something else to do."

Yeah, the distractions. I'd done that too.

I wasn't expecting any miracles with Peyton, though. He'd just arrived; he'd just met her for the first time, and he was already communicating with her. At the very least, it was a reason to make him an offer he couldn't refuse. Because if, in ten minutes, he could calm her down from a tantrum, imagine what he could do in a few months.

"You don't have to remember everything I said," he assured her. "I'll remind you, okay?"

She sniffled and shrugged, then nodded slightly.

"Did you see the amazing breakfast out there?" he asked next. "I think I'm gonna have pancakes. Do you like pancakes?"

She nodded, which wasn't technically a lie. She only happened to like them very rarely.

"Come on, then. Let's go eat. I'll show you how to make animals with the pancakes."

"What ammamal?"

I nodded to Cathryn, and we made our way back to the dining area.

I hoped this was a step in the right direction.

"I'm hiring him," I said quietly.

Cathryn dipped her chin and sat down. "He does seem to have a way about him. He jumped right in."

To say the least.

Knowing how sensitive Julia was right after a tantrum, both

Cathryn and I pretended to be immersed in our breakfast when she returned with Peyton in tow.

"May I have pancakes, please?" Peyton asked and took his seat.

I furrowed my brow at him. "Of course." They were right in front of him.

He quirked a grin and tilted his head at Julia. "Your turn to ask."

She scrunched her nose and eyed me. "Pancakes, pwlease."

"That was fucking awesome," Peyton stated bluntly.

Julia gasped at the curse and slapped a hand over her mouth before she giggled.

The sound made my goddamn heart soar, and it caused a rush of emotions to flow within me. I also understood his approach now. He was going to lead by example, something Julia had never had.

That morning, I was willing to bet I became the first boss to serve his future assistant pancakes.

He looked extremely satisfied. "Thank you."

I plated two pancakes for Julia too, and she mirrored him once again with a quiet, "Thank you."

CHAPTER

3.

"N ame your price for a minimum of one year of around-the-clock employment with me, because I'm not letting you go," I said as soon as we left the suite.

"A million dollars."

"Done."

"Dude, what the fuck. I was kidding."

"I wasn't." I pressed the button for the elevator and faced him. "But don't call me dude again. It's sir or Mr. Delamare." Then I handed him my work phone and a whole lot of information. "All work-related matters come through here. You're in charge of it. The code is sixty-four, thirty-four. You'll find my meetings and appointments in the calendar—which is synced with Mathis's calendar—same with birthdays and other reminders. And speaking of Mathis—you need to talk to him immediately so he can get you travel-ready for us." I paused briefly, moderately impressed with how he appeared to process everything without an ounce of confusion on his face. "Passwords and account details are in the app with a padlock on it. Every morning, I want a briefing of the day's schedule. A week's notice is required for birthdays, two days for private appointments, such as the doctor or dentist. Everything related to travels is Mathis's responsibility, so just coordinate with him."

"Yes, sir. Understood." He followed me into the elevator and rubbed his forehead. Under his arm, he carried a paper planner. I didn't know people used those these days. "But I was seriously kidding about the pay. I'd do it for half. Hell, I'd—"

"I would've paid the double." I shrugged. "You're not the best negotiator, are you?"

He shot me a frustrated look. "*Dude*. Halt. Stop. I was shooting blindly back there." He gestured toward the suite.

"Good aim."

"You don't get it. Are you sure you wanna hire someone who's never done this before? Even I'm on the fence, though not about the tasks—"

"What is it, then?" I wondered.

He released a breath and watched the elevator display flash with each floor we descended. "No amount of money will erase the fact that I've never been away from my family for more than two weeks at a time before," he said. "I can't fuck off for a whole year."

I frowned at him. "You don't think I will keep you away from them, do you? There are holidays and plenty of opportunities for you to fly out here for a quick visit."

"Oh. *Oh*." He appeared to have just lost an insurmountable weight off his shoulders. He shot me a dopey grin. "Do you think I'll be able to go home once a month? Like, just overnight or something like that."

I nodded slowly, thinking. "That would be your jet lag, not mine. But it should be doable. We have this week to negotiate the terms, then I want everything in writing."

"Copy that." He nodded and pinched his lips together, as if he was trying to hide his smile. It was sweet. "Can I ask you some questions in the car? I'd like to get to know you better so I can anticipate your needs."

Sweet Jesus, those were the magic words, weren't they?

"Sure." I exited the elevator and checked my watch. Right on time. Mathis should be outside waiting.

"Before our flight tomorrow, I want you to pull some quarterly reports from the hotels that've undergone renovations in the past ten years," I said, getting in the car. One meeting down, three to go. "The quarter before and two quarters after renovations. Start with the West Coast locations."

"Yes, sir."

I side-eyed him as he made notes in the planner. He had my phone open on the page too. "You're not going to ask if you need verification at headquarters?"

"No, sir," he replied. "A man looking for answers doesn't want questions." He slid me a little grin. "It's better I ask someone else about this. In short, I'll figure it out."

Hm. Interesting. He wasn't wrong, of course, but it was his first day. I'd never had an assistant before who hadn't been trained by the previous assistant.

That was a terrific phrase, however. *A man looking for answers doesn't want questions.* I bet Hilton would be sad to lose such a service-minded employee. I smiled to myself and peered out the window.

"Back to personal matters," he announced. "How do you like your coffee?"

"Black, simple. I'm not fussy when I'm traveling," I replied. "It irritates me when I'm in a lunch meeting and someone has to order an organic soy mocha latte with a double shot of vegan espresso. Christ. Just order black, with milk or sugar. Nobody wants to know that you only shower once a month or that your wife's put you on a new diet."

Peyton spluttered through a snicker and made a couple

27

notes. "Old-school with a passionate resentment toward hipsters."

I wasn't sure if he was joking or if he'd written that down, but he wasn't wrong this time either.

"You said you're not fussy when you're traveling," he went on. "What about when you're at home?"

"Same, almost. Black, very strong, but Cathryn introduced me to a hazelnut syrup I'll treat myself to. Just a splash of it."

He nodded slowly and jotted it down.

It filled me with contentment. A slow rush of warmth that settled over my chest.

"Any dietary restrictions or allergies?" he asked next.

"None, but I avoid fresh tomatoes if I can," I said. "The world's most overrated vegetable. It rarely belongs on the plate, if you ask me. Tomatoes should be crushed. I do like marinara and such, but for salads...?" I shuddered. "Don't get me started on burgers. Way to ruin a perfectly good meal."

I'd amused Peyton again for some reason.

My last meeting before lunch was a bit different. I'd spent my time in Seattle meeting with managers of our Washington locations, but one of our brands stood out in the statistics to the point where I'd requested to meet the man in charge of advertising.

It was for Westwater Wild, our line of hotels always located near nature. We'd launched the brand in 2009, if I remembered correctly, and it was one of the few lines that consistently performed well.

When Peyton and I arrived at the restaurant, Bennett Brooks was already there.

"It's an honor to meet you in person, Mr. Delamare."

I shook his hand firmly. "Likewise. I hope to learn a lot from you."

He was a handsome man with a kind smile, and he greeted Peyton too before we took our seats and ordered coffee.

"I understand you're a busy man, so I took the liberty of putting together a virtual tour of a selection of the Wild locations for you." Bennett extended a USB drive, and I gestured for Peyton to keep it. "You'll see the rooms up close, the front desk areas, the dining areas, as well as some of the exteriors we've used to distinguish the series."

"That's excellent, thank you," I replied. "My main question is, from a marketing point of view, why is Wild doing better than some of our more upscale brands?"

"May I be blunt?" he asked, with a hint of a British accent.

"I'd prefer it."

He cleared his throat and sat forward slightly. "I'm not sure it's about marketing. I believe it's partly due to the demographic. The guests at Wild are, well, not as demanding. Despite that we're nearing a decade since our agency helped you launch Wild, the hotels are still new and fresh. They were built for this specific theme. They're not old buildings that you bought to redesign or give a makeover."

I nodded pensively. "We're also fairly alone in this market, yes?"

Wild had been my baby once upon a time, a project I'd started working on when my grandfather became ill. I suspected it was the biggest reason he'd asked me to get more involved in the company, because he saw the originality of it as well. No other hotels catered to outdoor lovers the way we did. They didn't see the point, as backpackers and campers didn't tend to spend much money on hotels. Which was technically true.

However, if you controlled the market, those who did prefer staying in a hotel were essentially yours.

"Absolutely," Mr. Brooks replied with a nod. "But if we're discussing ratings, the demographic matters more because it's a group of travelers that doesn't demand as much comfort, something that reflects in how they respond to surveys and reviews. The hotel is a place to sleep before they explore the nearby hiking trails and so on. At a hotel for business travelers, you need to be the slice of heaven where guests can unwind from a long day."

"Of course." I glanced at the server as she arrived with our beverages, and then I processed what Mr. Brooks was telling me. None of it was new to me, but by pointing out how we catered to our guests, he made me wonder if we'd reached the point where we had to reinvent ourselves.

When we were alone again, I pressed forward. "It's an aging industry. We don't keep up with the new trends, partly because it's expensive. Renovations and alterations cost millions—per location. But the fact remains—we are losing the younger generation of business travelers to Airbnb and the like. Our target demographic is getting smaller, which creates a significant gap in our loyalty program. The seasoned business traveler stays on top. They're not likely to leave us. But we're not gaining new, hungry travelers who want to collect the rewards like they used to." I leaned forward and took a sip of my coffee. "And I think that affects the ratings too. We have a young generation that follows their superiors into chain hotels—maybe they sign up for our loyalty program—they try it out, and they're disappointed. Their friends tell them about cost-effective alternatives, and so, they leave."

Bennett appeared well-read on the topic; he nodded along and added his own two cents. "It's the same generation that prefers to fly with low-cost carriers. Messenger bags are replacing the briefcases."

I chuckled. "Too true."

"So it means it's uncharted territory for upscale chain hotels," he noted. "Our agency did a local campaign for JetBlue last year, and I'm convinced there are plenty of opportunities to appeal to their travelers. But you do have to renew some of your locations in order to advertise them well. Proximity and comfort aren't listed as highly on the list of priorities anymore. It's technology and communication."

I hummed. He was giving me much to consider, and I wanted him on board. I wanted his agency to propose changes and team up with our in-house marketing department.

I requested a quiet place for lunch once I felt my energy draining out of me and a headache settling in. I left it to Peyton and Mathis to decide, and our Seattle resident suggested a seafood place not too far from here.

"It should be empty by now." Peyton checked his watch. "Yeah, the rush is over."

He was right, and we were shown into an oasis in the middle of the financial district. The restaurant sat in between two banks and had its own courtyard for outdoor dining in the back.

"Excellent choice." I clapped Peyton on the shoulder before I took my seat. The area was essentially a greenhouse with its glass ceiling, vines, and potted plants everywhere. Best of all, only three of the dozen or so tables were occupied. "When's my next meeting?"

"Not until four thirty."

Good, we could turn this into a long lunch, then. I wanted

to discuss some terms with Peyton, and I needed a bit of down-time to let my mind rest.

I ordered a vodka with my lunch and noticed Peyton hesitating as he scanned his menu, so I mustered a smile and told him not to let me drink alone.

"Heh." That seemed to settle it for him, and he ordered a glass of white wine with his scallops. "I wasn't around to enjoy the three-martini lunch era."

I lifted my brows. "Are you implying that I'm old, Peyton?"

"No." He smiled sweetly, a little *too* sweetly. "You're...seasoned?"

I huffed a chuckle, enjoying his firecracker attitude. I didn't get to experience it often.

At another time in my life, playful submissives had been my heroin.

Not that my success rate in that arena had given me anything lasting either. If anything, it was the infatuation of what could've been that I clung to. The reality had looked far bleaker, and aside from a few wonderful, temporary arrangements without deeper feelings involved, I'd left the BDSM world the same way I'd entered it—alone.

"Hey, I was kidding."

"What?" I glanced up from my lap, smoothing out my napkin, and it took me a second to realize he'd misinterpreted my silence for offense. He had no reason to look contrite. "Oh, of course." I smiled in reassurance. "I'm not easily offended, and everyone knows not to listen to Generation Z."

"*Whoa.*" He sat back and stared at me, his hands resting on the table. "That's harsh, man. I'm a millennial."

"I wouldn't brag about that either, little one." I spotted the server approaching with our drinks, finally. "Stop looking so constipated. Our drinks are here."

I quenched my immediate thirst with half a glass of water

before I took a much-needed swig of my vodka. The lemon had to go, but the ice stayed.

"I was going to ask if you wanted me to make any plans for your birthday in a few weeks, but now I won't," Peyton told me. "And forty-five is a pretty big birthday."

"I'm sorry, I wasn't listening. Did you say something?" I stifled my smirk when he stewed in silence, perhaps torn between professionalism and what he wanted to say. But as fun as banter could be, I had something more important to discuss. "Let's talk terms, Peyton. I want to make you mine as soon as possible."

He chuckled at my intentional phrasing, and fuck me if his ears didn't tint red. What a sight.

His carefree manner made me want to play with him. Push him a bit. I'd already gotten away with calling him little one...

What else could I get away with?

The vodka left a trail of heat down my throat and loosened me up slightly.

"Well..." He cleared his throat and shifted in his seat. "I'm willing to give you a year with little to no breaks, other than that I'd like to be able to see my mom and sister once a month—give or take. I, uh, I also need to step out twice a month to record my radio show." Oh, right. I'd forgotten about that part. "I asked my boss at WX, and he will make arrangements for me to be able to record them locally in Boston instead—with their parent company."

"I'll have to listen in sometime," I said. "It's about history, yes?"

He nodded. "Yes, sir. It's the only thing I have that I'm actually educated for. I'd like to keep that job for as long as it's possible."

I tilted my head. "What did you study in college?"

"History and education," he responded. "I'm a high school

teacher." He shrugged with one shoulder. "There're no jobs available where I want to work, though."

Interesting. I had to admit I didn't see that one coming. "You're very service-minded. I assumed you'd studied hospitality management or customer service."

"That's part of why I'm not in any rush to find a teaching job," he said. "I'm...I'm tired, to be honest. I've been mentally exhausted for several years. Being there for my sister—being alone with her, having all that responsibility...it's been taxing. Then my mom needed a lot of help when we got her back into our lives too. It's not until now—or the last two years—I've been able to venture out on my own." He played with the stem of his wineglass. "I always knew I wanted to be a teacher eventually, so I forced myself to stay in school and get my degree. But as soon as I saw there were no open positions in my hometown, I sort of just walked away. I needed a job where I didn't have to be in charge." He seemingly felt the need to add something quickly. "I have no issues working my ass off. I like challenges and having a lot to do. I just don't want to be responsible for hundreds of students. That career path will be there when I'm ready."

A lot to unpack there, to put it mildly. I adjusted my tie, finding myself uncomfortable with...something. He tugged at a chord in me, and I wasn't sure I liked it. He was tired and didn't want to lead. He wanted to follow orders. How could I not be drawn to that like a moth to a flame? How could I not want to take a step closer and... Fuck. No. This was not the time for me to give the caregiver in me a voice. I'd buried that part of me. Or rather, it was reserved for Julia, in a very different way from how I once manifested my need to take care of those dear to me.

"That wasn't supposed to be some word vomit." Peyton rubbed the back of his neck, then reached for his wine and chugged half the glass.

I winced. That wasn't how one enjoyed that wine.

"Feel free to word-vomit, as you so eloquently put it, anytime," I told him. "But do let me know when we've reached 'another day' for the story of when your mother was missing for six years but then returned. I admit I'm curious."

He sent me a forced smile and nodded once. "I'll let you know. But...so, yeah, those are my terms. I wanna be able to see my family and record my show. The rest of the time..." He trailed off.

"You're mine," I finished with a faint grin.

He huffed and shook his head at me, eyes showing the amusement he tried to hide. "Maybe I should ask if you have any weird requests."

"Maybe you should."

Our food was on its way, so I ignored Peyton's narrowed-eyed look. But God, it was fun to tease him. I wanted much more of it.

I nodded in thanks at the server, peering down at my seafood linguine. It smelled fantastic, and I ordered more wine for us before she left. Because a meal like this was supposed to be enjoyed with wine.

"What you did with Julia this morning," I said, tucking into my meal, "with the mirroring. The way you encouraged her to follow your lead—I want more of that. She doesn't have any siblings, and I think it would be a good way for her to learn how to be more polite."

"Okay." He nodded. "Yeah, it seemed to work the first time anyway. I'm sure it'll be trial and error a whole lot."

Definitely.

I went further. "Well, we'll try it—at least once a day. You ask me for permission, politely, and we'll urge her to follow. Don't forget to include her title for me."

Peyton dropped his fork. It landed on his plate with a clank.

I smothered my smile and let a thrill travel its course through my body, and I took a swig of my water.

"You want me to do what?" he asked quietly.

"What I want is for *her* to get into the habit of saying 'May I,' 'Please,' and 'Thank you, Daddy.'"

He was blushing.

Unfortunately, I wasn't a complete asshole, and I wanted to give him one out. "Unless it makes you too uncomfortable, of course."

"No, it's okay," he mumbled into his wine. "It's for Julia."

Oh no, sweet boy, that one is for me.

My daughter had no issues calling me Daddy. She just happened to use it as an accusation or protest most of the time these days.

The server returned with a bottle for us—and waited for my approval of it—and then, while she poured me a glass and refilled Peyton's, I tried to come up with more things I wanted in writing. If I could somehow involve touching—innocently, naturally—I'd have something to look forward to. Something to apply to my fantasies. Something that wouldn't result in a sexual harassment case.

I cringed internally. What was wrong with me? Was I that depraved?

Yes. Yes, I was.

But that wasn't an excuse for what I was doing. I had to quit. I had to be professional.

Peyton pulled out my work phone from his pocket and swiped the screen. "Mathis forwarded the flight information for tomorrow." He glanced up at me. "I've completely forgotten that I need to pack. Do you mind if I head home after work?"

"Of course not. Take a few hours, have dinner with your family or something."

He shook his head. "Mathis is going to help me get some

PreCheck stuff sorted for the airport, so I'll just call them. Mom already knows I'm taking the job. She's excited for me."

"You don't live together," I stated rather than asked. I'd gotten the impression he wasn't originally from Seattle but lived here now.

"No, they're back in my hometown. It's a couple hours north of here."

"I understand."

"I'm not giving up my studio, though," he went on. "It took me forever to get a lease of my own, and it's not crazy expensive."

Well, that was his choice, of course. He could afford it, now more than ever.

"By the way, could you help me pick out some work clothes?" he asked. I furrowed my brow, caught off guard, at which he continued in a bit of a rush. "I only have this suit and one other. At Hilton, I didn't need more. I was supposed to look the same every day anyway, you know? But there're some stores nearby—where your next meeting is, I mean—and I thought... Never mind. I shouldn't have asked."

The fire within reignited instantly, and it blazed through me. He damn well knew it wasn't a normal request. It wasn't something you asked of your boss. Unless he had a second agenda that he was hiding very poorly, much like me. Was that even possible? Could it be?

"I have a better idea." I wiped my mouth on my napkin and did my best to rein in the hope. "When we get to LA tomorrow, I'll take you to the best tailor on the West Coast."

"Really?" It was precious how he perked up.

I nodded and reached for my wine, picturing it. Him on that small podium, me seated in a nearby chair, watching. Fuck, how I would watch him.

"Thank you." He smiled, the relief evident. His eyes were

incredibly expressive, not to mention intoxicatingly sexy. "I mean, you obviously have great taste in business fashion, so I figured I'd be in good hands."

My hands were absolutely good.

I almost told him he'd be safe with me, but what a lie that would've been. He was anything but safe with me.

CHAPTER 4.

I woke up the next morning to Julia's fingers wandering across my face.

Bracing myself for whatever mood she could be in, I turned my face into her touch and kissed her palm.

"Morning, baby."

"Hi." She poked my nose.

So far, so good. She wasn't smiling, but she wasn't upset either.

I soaked in the sight of her. Her big blue eyes, the messy waves giving her an impressive bed head, her chubby cheeks, her dimples... The dimples came from her mother.

"You are so beautiful. You know that?" I stroked her cheek gently.

I secretly loved traveling with her because it brought me closer to her. She slept in my bed, and there was no room she could close herself into.

She scrunched her little button nose, but her eyes brimmed with mirth. "Nuh-uh."

"It's true," I said, stretching out on my back. I placed a hand under my head and yawned. "Before you were born, we decided that you were going to be the most beautiful girl in the world, and we were right."

She huffed and crawled up on my chest, planting her butt on my stomach. "Wheu's the boy? My new fwriend?"

"Peyton?" I smiled at her declaration. "He will be here soon. He's coming with us on the plane today."

"Okay. I gots to pee now."

"All right. I better help you, then." I chuckled and followed her into the ensuite bath. "Do you want to take a bath now or after we fly?"

"Not now," she protested.

"Okay, we'll do it later." I quickly changed the topic in an attempt to thwart her worsening mood. "What do you want for breakfast?"

Wrong question. She let out a grunt and pushed at me, then started crying.

Fuck.

By the time Peyton arrived, having slept in a hotel room a floor below us, Julia had been bawling for a solid hour. She wanted breakfast, but she didn't want breakfast. She positively seethed at the sight of a yellow dress Cathryn picked out for her, resulting in a tantrum that catapulted a headache into my skull.

I packed our bags while Cathryn dealt with dressing Julia.

"Can I try something?" Peyton asked, dropping his bag at the door. A duffel. We would get him proper luggage, I decided.

"No need to ask." I gestured for the bedroom I'd shared with Julia.

He ducked into the room and greeted Julia. "Hey, you! I told you I'd be back, didn't I?"

"Nooo!" Julia whined through her cries. "I don't wanna!"

"Oh, but we do. Come on, sweetheart. Let's find you some clothes."

I peered into the room just as Peyton picked up Julia and positioned her on his hip. Then he discarded a pile of clothes on the bed, leaving two dresses behind.

"I like these two the best," he said. "But maybe the purple one a little more. I'm right, aren't I?"

She hiccuped and sniffled, wiping at her cheeks.

"I know I'm right." He gave her tear-stained cheek a smooch. "It's a great day for a purple dress."

"'Kay," she whimpered.

I sent Cathryn a pensive look, because I understood what he was doing, and it seemed so simple. He'd done the same thing yesterday. He was eliminating the majority of the choices. He was making it easier for her.

Jesus Christ. I scrubbed a hand over my mouth and jaw. Could that be it?

I observed Peyton's carefree assertiveness while he helped Julia get dressed. He spoke with conviction and kept things light at the same time. He was certain we'd have a good time in Los Angeles, and then he revealed that his favorite flavor of ice cream was strawberry swirl.

"What do you like?" He turned the question on her. "You can choose between, umm..." He tapped his chin, pretending to think. "Chocolate ice cream and *vegetable* ice cream."

Julia didn't know what to do with herself. She squeaked, part amused, part upset, and flailed her way into the dress. "Focolate! Can't have veggie ice cwream!"

"Are you *sure*?" Peyton narrowed his eyes suspiciously. "In LA, they eat all kinds of weird shit."

"*Silly*." Julia palmed her face, exasperated. And cuter than I could ever describe.

My God. I drummed my fingers across my lips, and Cathryn joined me in the doorway.

"He's removing her options," she whispered.

I nodded.

I felt like an utter fool for not trying that route before. I didn't dare believe that this was some magic solution to everything, but perhaps it was one adjustment out of many that would help.

The strategy I'd tried—one of them, but the one closest to Peyton's—was a period during which I decided everything. I'd picked her clothes, her food, her cartoons. And perhaps that had been a step too far, because she'd only fought me. Whatever I had said yes to had prompted a stubborn no from her.

Peyton was guiding her. He gave her some wiggle room so as to not box her in; he engaged with her.

Amazing.

"I think we're ready," Peyton declared, smiling down at Julia. "How about you and I go running in the hall while Daddy and Cathryn do the boring packing?"

"Yes!" Julia was on board.

And I was on board with him calling me Daddy.

"I don't need my passport, right?" Peyton asked. "I mean, I brought it, but I read that my driver's license is enough."

"For domestic travel," I confirmed with a nod. I gestured for the PreCheck lane and side-eyed him. "Have you flown before? You mentioned going to LA."

He shook his head, his gaze flickering all over the place. From the signs and the roped-off area, to the TSA agents and the travelers up ahead who were placing laptops in the containers.

"I drove," he replied.

My mouth twitched. He was endearingly lost at the

moment, and I couldn't help myself. I gave his neck a gentle squeeze and murmured, "Follow my lead."

Mathis and Cathryn were behind us, and I could trust her to take care of Julia. She was, ironically, the easiest child to bring along for air travel.

Given that Peyton had checked his only piece of luggage, we went through security without a hitch. All he had to do was place his planner and two phones with my iPad.

"They didn't tell me to take off my shoes," he said as we continued toward our gate. "A buddy of mine gave me a heads-up about shoes and sometimes belts."

"That's if you fly economy."

We reached the gate just a couple minutes before it was time for us to board. For this part, Julia wanted to be with me, and I handed over my briefcase to Peyton.

"I'd fly with you every day if it gets you in my arms." I pressed a kiss to her hair as she locked her arms around my neck.

"That was the sweetest thing I've ever heard," Peyton said quietly.

"Don't sound so surprised," I drawled. "I'm a sweet man."

Cathryn snorted behind me.

I shot her a narrowed-eyed look.

Mere minutes later, I was no longer Julia's favorite. She wanted back to Cathryn as soon as we'd boarded, so the ladies took their seats two rows behind Peyton and me, and Mathis had his seat on the other side of the aisle. He liked his privacy.

"I'll get my shit together soon," Peyton promised with an apology in his voice. "First time—I'm just nervous."

"It's quite all right," I assured him. "Would you like a distraction?"

He nodded jerkily.

I shrugged out of my suit jacket, and a flight attendant

whooshed by to grab it. "In a few hours, you'll be modeling shirts for me."

Peyton whipped his head my way and stared blankly.

I smiled. "I understand, it's your first time. I'll be gentle. At first."

And there was the blush. It crept into place slowly, and he diverted his stare to the seat in front of him. I watched his Adam's apple shift with his swallow. Christ, he was dangerous. He didn't seem to know it either.

"I don't get you." He spoke under his breath. "Either you have the most wicked sense of humor, or you're dead serious."

I chuckled.

"I've never had a boss like you, that's for sure," he finished.

That made me hum. "I've never had an assistant like you either."

Approximately four hours later, I was about to get what I craved.

With Cathryn and Julia catching some rest at the hotel, Peyton and I had gone straight from the airport to Antonino's in Bel Air.

It was like traveling back in time to enter his shop. He was an old man, but he'd probably outlive his four sons, all of whom worked with him. He smoked, he drank, he denied his arthritis, and he'd shoot anyone who talked shit about Frank Sinatra. A series of pictures of the singer hung on the wall above the wide doorway leading to the private dressing rooms.

In all the recent years I'd come here when I was in town, he managed to squeeze in a spiel about how America was no longer free because he couldn't smoke in his own store. But to this day, the faint smell of cigars lingered in the cherry paneling on the walls.

"'Course I remember you, Ed," Antonino scoffed when I extended my hand. "Don't be stupid."

I smiled. "Good to see you again. I brought my assistant today. He's in need of a new wardrobe." I turned a bit and peered into the adjoining store next door where they sold everything a businessman could need. "I'm thinking one bespoke three-piece, two tailored regular suits, and a selection of shirts. He's got black covered."

"All right," the man grunted and gave Peyton a once-over. "Well, let's head to the back, boy." Then he hollered toward the clothing store section. "Mikey! Come give this kid a gander. I want ten shirts to go with the new indigo we got in last week, and..." He tilted his head from side to side, studying Peyton. "Let's go with dark and medium gray. Charcoal and the iron one, Mikey!"

"Yeah, yeah, I hear ya, Pop!" Mikey hollered back.

"*Bene.* Let's go."

We followed Antonino to the back where he had his dressing room, and I breathed in the scents of cigar, cherry wood, and leather. Antonino's son joined us for a brief moment to guesstimate Peyton's size before disappearing again.

I was only here to enjoy the show, so I took a seat in one of the two big leather chairs.

Antonino snapped his fingers and pointed to the round podium in the center of the floor, silently telling Peyton to get up there. "How long're you in town this time, Ed?"

"Just a week, but we'll be back in the beginning of June," I replied. "Do you think you can squeeze in his second fitting before we leave?"

"Eh. Sure. Should work." He lowered his glasses from the

45

top of his head and grabbed his measuring tape. "Want me to keep his patterns on file?"

"Please do." If I got my way, we'd be back here.

Noticing that Peyton was trying to get my attention, I met his gaze, and he mouthed "You're crazy" to me. Then he rubbed his fingers together, indicating that it was going to be a costly visit.

I merely flashed him a smirk.

It might come as a surprise to him later to learn that I didn't have any expensive hobbies or much to spend money on. My lifestyle was far from cheap, naturally, but I didn't indulge out of boredom. I wasn't nuts about gadgets. I didn't have a yacht or a garage full of cars. I had one. One car. And a motorcycle I hadn't ridden since Julia was born.

I didn't golf, I wasn't part of some ridiculous country club, I didn't know how to sail, I couldn't play any instruments, so there was no fancy grand piano at home...

I liked to fish, but I hadn't gone in years.

Now Peyton was in my life, however temporarily, and I felt like spending some money on him.

Sue me.

When Antonino was done measuring and his son had wheeled in a garment rack, we were left alone for a bit to decide on shirts, what needed to be taken in, and some fabric samples. But in my experience, it was best to let Antonino decide. He was a fantastic craftsman who'd been doing this for over fifty years.

"Well, what are you waiting for?" I leaned back in my chair and folded one leg over the other.

Antonino had closed the sliding doors, much to my satisfaction.

"This is mildly terrifying," Peyton muttered. He stepped

down from the podium and flipped through the selection of shirts. "I don't know which one to choose."

"You'll try all of them, and then we'll see which ones are keepers."

He'd taken off his suit jacket and shoes while Antonino had taken his measurements. Now I just needed Peyton to remove the rest of his clothes.

He glanced at me hesitantly. "Are you really going to watch?"

"Unless it makes you uncomfortable." I used the same words I'd used yesterday.

He mumbled something under his breath that I couldn't hear, but then he started unbuttoning his shirt.

I drew a deep breath and rested my arms along the armrests.

Only thing missing, really, was a cigar. Perhaps a glass of whiskey too.

He draped his white shirt over the rack and brushed his fingers along the items Antonino's son had selected. Peyton had such a stunning body, but I was an idiot for hoping I'd see more of it. Of course he wore an undershirt, and he had no reason to take it off.

It made me abandon my chair and take charge. I walked over to him and picked a dark navy shirt for him. "This will look good with a gray suit." Wasting no time, I ushered him up onto the podium and joined him there, where I finally got my hands on him. I was all business, keeping my personal pleasure about this to myself. "We'll need some ties and cuff links for you as well." I smoothed down the fabric along his arms, then his chest —my God, his chest—and helped him button the shirt. "What do you think?" I gestured to the full-length mirror a few feet behind him.

He turned around and inspected the shirt.

I subtly checked out his ass under the guise of tucking the shirt into his dress pants.

"I like it. It feels amazing." Peyton twisted his body in the mirror to study his profile, and I clenched my jaw. What were the odds of him actually not being straight? I'd banked on it earlier. Now I was having doubts. "Is it weird that I'm excited about owning a three-piece? They're so classy." He gave me a quick glance. "You wore one the first time we met."

I inclined my head. "They place you one level above everyone else."

"How did you find me?" He faced me fully and unbuttoned his shirt.

I didn't meet his gaze. I wasn't embarrassed by any means; I was just busy drinking in the sight of his body. "The radio show provided me with your name and what you did for a living. Someone at the office in Boston handled the rest." I took the shirt from him and picked another, this time a light lavender one. Again, it would look great with the medium gray suit, and perhaps with a darker shade lavender tie. Peyton could pull off the color. I couldn't. "You could be a model," I murmured. "Perfect fit."

He exhaled a chuckle. "I'm too short."

He wasn't. He was average, around five ten or so, but perhaps too short for that profession. Repeating the motions from the last fitting, I smoothed my hands down his chest until I felt his abs clench under my touch.

He was going to drive me insane.

"You're tall, sir," he noted, peering up at me.

My jaw tensed, and I inspected the sleeve length. He couldn't be straight. Not if he was letting me do this. Noting that I was tall? Adorable. He was about as professional as I was.

"Try the green shirt," I commanded quietly. The dark color would enhance the gorgeous green of his eyes.

"Yes, sir."

I forced myself to return to the chair, wondering if there was actually a possibility I might eventually have him naked and spread out for me on my bed.

CHAPTER
5.

As predicted, Peyton's influence on Julia wasn't an instant fix, but I *did* believe there was significant improvement. Cathryn and I adopted his strategy to remove most of Julia's options, only keeping a select few for her, and it had eliminated several of her tantrums.

She was still at a sensitive age, but at least I wasn't making it worse for her anymore.

I'd been up early to work out in the gym, so I didn't see Julia until it was time for breakfast and she waltzed out of our bedroom, hand in hand with Peyton.

He was suited up and wore a little smirk for me. "Morning, Daddy."

Fuck.

"Mownin', Daddy!" Julia echoed.

"Good morning, you two." I touched her cheek before she crawled up into her booster seat. "Cathryn should be here soon. She stepped out to buy some fun things for your beach day."

It was a shame we'd be heading inland when we flew up to Santa Rosa the day after tomorrow, but we'd be back soon enough. Julia positively adored going to the beach. Her daddy was looking forward to a trip to wine country, however.

"Peyton come wid me to the beach?" Julia asked, nodding.

"Not today, darling. But you know what? We have the whole weekend off, both Saturday and Sunday. How about going to the pool together?" It was only a white lie. I had plenty of work, but I could do most of it poolside.

Julia was disgruntled but didn't push the matter.

Peyton served her a plate of fruit and a yogurt cup before taking a seat to eat the same thing. Julia scrunched her nose at it, but when she noticed Peyton's identical breakfast, she stuck a grape in her mouth.

The relief was indescribable.

How had I not figured it out sooner? She wanted someone to follow while going through this delicate time. I'd scoured bookstores for material on the development of toddlers. Perhaps she needed it even more now while we were traveling and structure wasn't a given.

Regardless, I was incredibly grateful for Peyton.

At noon, I was treated to a tour of one of our flagship hotels in downtown LA.

It was one of our most popular locations, and ratings were excellent. And yet, it wasn't supposed to be any different from our two similar hotels in Manhattan, both of which had shown a decline in ratings regarding service and amenities.

Were business travelers arriving in LA expecting less here, or was our staff in New York not as good?

Sophia, the front office manager, showed Peyton and me around the premises, from the two gyms—one on the eighteenth floor, one on the third—to the restaurants, from the rooms to the pool area on the roof. It was a large hotel. I'd stayed here before, though it'd been years. I preferred our smaller location in Santa Monica, partly because it was easier to get to LAX from there.

The downtown hotel was popular due to its proximity to convention centers and the fact that it was in the business district.

"And here, as you can see, we have our conference rooms," Sophia said as we exited the elevator on the seventeenth floor. "We have many tech travelers coming in from Silicon Valley, so we try to accommodate their needs."

Peyton stepped forward and handed me a Post-it.

Customer surveys show ratings in service have improved since she started working here two years ago.

I inclined my head in thanks before returning my attention to Sophia. "That's good. We're trying to lure them away from Airbnb in many of our other cities. So far, without much luck."

"Personalization, I believe, is key," Sophia responded. "Travelers are sharing their experiences on social media today, and there's nothing new and exciting about a hotel that looks the same in every city."

She had a point.

We passed all the conference rooms; big and small, some were occupied, some not.

"We have luck on our side," Sophia went on. "Many guests staying here require space for meetings, for instance. Airbnb won't help you there."

I furrowed my brow. That wasn't *luck*. It was a well-planned move to provide conference rooms in all major chain hotels.

I let the comment slide.

The tour ended in the executive lounge next to the gym on the eighteenth floor, where Sophia spoke of another change they'd made recently—to offer privacy in the lounge for smaller meetings. She proceeded to tell me she'd taken the liberty of arranging a "nook" for me with coffee and pastries as well as some reports from their in-house surveys.

"Thank you." It would be nice to get off my feet for a moment. The lounge was almost empty at this hour, and the dark oak wood dividers offered further seclusion. Two low couches and a table filled the little area, and a woman from the lounge staff came to pour our coffee as I sat down.

Then the women left.

"Want me to sort through these, sir?" Peyton sat down across from me and grabbed the stack of papers. "There's no need for you to read what we've already had access to." He rubbed his forehead and winced, which stole my attention much quicker than the surveys ever could.

"Are you all right?" I asked.

"Yeah, just a headache. Oh, wait. I have something for you." He patted his pockets and produced a very small flask.

My eyebrows went up. "It's a bit early, don't you think?"

He grinned quickly and poured a splash into my coffee. "It's hazelnut syrup. Cathryn helped me find it in a store."

Christ. That did something to me. I reached forward and took a tentative sip, and I felt the strong coffee mingling with a bit of hazelnutty sweetness.

"Good?" He cocked his head.

He looked so innocent. Sweeter than the syrup. Yet, undeniably sexy and far from harmless. Peyton wasn't new in the world. He had to know of the effect he could have on others. On me.

"Better." I took another sip and held his gaze. "I want you to kneel at my feet."

"Wh..." He shut up and swallowed hard. Shock was evident in his expression.

I refused to backtrack. I wanted him to sit on the floor, right here, right now, between my legs. "Come." I picked up the stack of papers on the table and left them on the couch next to me. Then I parted my legs a bit and waited patiently.

He rose from the couch with an unsteady breath.

I pushed the table forward once he'd stepped to the side, and I patted the edge of the cushion between my thighs. "Down here."

He stepped over my leg and stared at the floor. "Um."

"No ums. Sit, boy."

He cursed under his breath and sank to the floor, folding his legs underneath him.

Desire pooled in my lower body. The sense of control slithered into my veins, a heady feeling I'd missed terribly. I couldn't hold back any longer.

"There we go." I threaded my fingers through his soft hair and drew a deep breath. "Rest your head on my leg. Relax for a moment. Shut everything out."

He needed a break. He was already tending to my needs professionally better than anyone had before, and I was a demanding bastard.

It took him some time to relax, understandably, but I witnessed the tension leaving him slowly but surely. He sank lower to the floor and rested his cheek on my leg, facing away from me, and I kept combing my fingers through his hair, scratching his scalp and rubbing his neck.

Letting the silence stretch between us, I picked up one of the reports and went back to work for a while. The guests at this hotel were satisfied with our staff's service, and I was beginning to wonder if I could somehow orchestrate an exchange program. Say, send a team from our New York hotels out here and vice versa. Perhaps they could spend a few weeks learning how things worked at a different location.

I wanted Bennett Brooks's opinion on the matter, because this should have some value in advertising as well. Everything was showcased on social media these days. An arena we had yet to join actively, other than providing customer support via Facebook and Twitter.

I'd have to set up a meeting with Three Dots, the agency where Bennett worked, and our in-house department.

Peyton shifted on the floor, and I lifted the papers to see him. He was turning around. He blinked sleepily and rested his other cheek on my leg, granting me a view of his beautiful face.

"I don't know what you're doing to me," he mumbled with his eyes closed, "but don't stop."

I suppressed the rumble that emanated from my chest and rubbed his neck affectionately. "I have no intention of stopping, pet."

He shivered violently and sighed in contentment.

Sweet boy.

I set down the reports and adjusted my cock.

———————

Our location in Santa Rosa sat on the outskirts of the city and was geared toward wine country visitors. It'd been built to give the guests a vineyard feel, and the main building only had twenty rooms. The rest of the accommodations were made up of villas.

Mathis usually preferred to make his own reservations; he had friends all over the world and liked to meet up with them when he had time off. But here, he would stay with us. I'd picked a villa near the pool area for Julia's sake, and the weather was on our side. It was going to be a warm weekend.

With one villa consisting of two suites, each with a terrace that had a view of the pool, it was no question that Julia and I would take one, and Mathis and Cathryn would share the other.

The question was where Peyton would end up, and I had my hopes.

"Talk about the royal treatment." Peyton carried a sleepy Julia into our suite and eyed the coffee table in the living room. There was champagne in an ice bucket, a chocolate assortment, and a tray with cheese and crackers. "Look at this, sweetheart. I think the animal crackers are for you."

"Best part of traveling with the boss," Mathis said, entering the bedroom to set down our luggage. "All the free stuff."

"It's not my charming personality?" I asked, amused.

He laughed, clapped me on the back, and headed out the door.

He'd been with me too long. No one respected me anymore. I chuckled to myself and joined Peyton and Julia in the living room. It was going to be a good weekend; I could feel it.

"Wheu's Cathryn?" Julia asked.

"Next door. She's just going to unpack, and then she's taking *you*—" I poked her belly "—to the pool."

She grinned tiredly. "Okay, good. No nap today. I wanna swim."

"Yeah, you don't look sleepy at all," I laughed softly.

She shook her head furiously.

"Well, I'll go unpack our bags." I leaned forward and pressed a kiss to her forehead, at the same time sneaking in a small touch at Peyton's lower back. Then I headed for the bedroom.

———

That evening, I had Peyton make reservations in the hotel restaurant for only the two of us. I met him outside after I'd printed out my proposal in the office.

Gossip traveled quickly, and everyone on the premises in a

Westwater uniform appeared to know I was staying here. We were shown to a table in the outdoor seating area of the cantina-inspired restaurant, overlooking the blossoming fields to the north. It was the second most popular time of year to visit Northern California, so the establishment was fairly packed.

The thought struck me when I spotted all the flickering candles on the tables that this was a couples' resort. Which explained why Julia had complained about the lack of children at the pool earlier. Technically, I'd known this before. It just hadn't meant anything until I sat down with Peyton across from me.

Heaters, thick blankets, and wine kept everyone around us warm, and I wasn't the only one picking up on the romantic atmosphere. Fuck, it hadn't been intentional. Peyton cleared his throat and glanced at the couple closest to us, then shifted in his seat and opened his menu.

I decided not to say anything, not to make any excuses. It was only dinner.

Wine. I needed wine.

We listened to the recommendations of the chef and the sommelier, and we received our drinks instantly. I suspected one of the servers would have their eyes on us the whole time.

It made me wish for privacy.

There were a select few couples Peyton was watching more than the others. Gay couples.

"You're thinking hard on something," I noted.

Peyton flushed and took a sip of his wine. Curious reaction. "Sorry. It's very beautiful here."

He didn't want to share. Fair enough.

"I wanted to discuss our contract," I revealed. "Rather, a different contract."

"Oh? I thought we already..."

I nodded. We had finalized the details for his employment

with the company as well as his private employment with me for watching Julia.

"This one would between you and me," I said. "A set of... requests, if you will. Rules."

"Rules," he stated quietly.

I tucked my napkin under the table and smiled faintly. "I think you can guess I have some unconventional interests."

I didn't think he could get sexier, but the candlelight did it. The shadows enhanced the pink flush of his cheeks in the most exquisite way, and his green eyes took on a fiery glint.

"I want your signature on the contract," I told him, "but it would be symbolic. You can back out anytime you want."

He licked his lips nervously. "Can I see it?"

"Of course." I pushed down my own nerves and reached into the inner pocket of my suit. It was something I'd worked on during our flight up here. "It's pretty straightforward and short."

"Nothing about you is straightforward and short," he muttered, accepting the piece of paper.

I grinned into my wineglass. This, I had to see. Him, reading my wishes, and then, hearing his response.

I'd listed five items. Five things I wanted to do, or I wanted him to do, and that was all. I wouldn't push him beyond that. Instead, I was hoping he'd come to me. I was hoping he'd be so desperate that he couldn't help himself anymore. Because I wouldn't budge an inch.

"You—you wanna dress me?" He looked up from the paper, eyes wide.

"Yes."

He swallowed hard and read from the draft. "You wanna dress me every morning, you want me to kneel at your feet once a day if privacy can be guaranteed, you want—wait. You wanna put sunscreen on me?"

"When we're in the Caribbean." I nodded slightly.

I needed my hands on him.

"I, uh..." He coughed and squirmed in his seat. "You also want me to sit across from you whenever we fly private." Which we would be doing when we went to the Caribbean. If it weren't for the new environmental policy Westwater went public with last year, we'd fly private more frequently. "And you don't want me to ask why you want all this."

"In fact, not a single word of it," I emphasized. Because words were a valve. Valves released pressure. I didn't want anything released until it was my cock buried balls deep in his ass. "You either agree, or you don't. Completely your choice. If you say yes, you will take a journey with me. If you say no, anything else still stands. This doesn't affect your employment with me whatsoever."

It was a journey I believed he was curious about.

Whether or not he was brave enough to take the leap was up to him.

Our food arrived, and I wasn't expecting a response right this minute anyway. Peyton was, to put it mildly, flustered. He folded the draft of the contract with trembling fingers, and I took it—just in case. We didn't need a breeze to blow it off the table and have someone else catch it and see what it said.

"Wait—what're you... I mean... I haven't said no."

I smothered the explosion of joy and satisfaction, and I pocketed the contract again. "Let me know when you agree, then."

He took a piece of garlic bread from the basket but didn't eat it. He seemed more intent on breaking it into tiny little pieces and feeding them to his paella.

"Unconventional," he mumbled under his breath. "I'll say."

I smiled around a forkful of paella—fantastic paella, I might add—and enjoyed witnessing his discomfort. He wanted it. I was certain. *Come to me, little boy.* What a world of pleasure I wanted to show him. I'd never stood a chance against his allure.

"Fuck it." He threw the last of his shredded bread onto his plate and reached for his napkin. "I agree to it. I say yes. What do I need to do?"

I chewed slowly, allowing the desire to settle like a blanket over me. The feeling of power followed, and I relished it. After taking a sip of my wine, I pulled out the contract again, with a pen this time, and slid both across the table.

"Just sign here."

CHAPTER 6.

Considering I was spending the weekend comparing reports and surveys between our American and European hotels while never venturing far from the pool area, I went easy on Peyton those first two days.

He spent most of the time with Julia anyway, so he was either in swim trunks or casual wear. There wasn't a chance he was ready for me to get involved in helping him into the trunks, resulting in just a quick moment where I watched him put on jeans and a tee.

There was also no privacy granted for me to indulge in having him at my feet during our entire stay in Santa Rosa.

It wasn't until we arrived in San Francisco and to our West Coast headquarters there that I got a moment alone with him. We borrowed an office to go through our contracts one more time, and he kneeled next to my chair until it was time to sign.

"Up you go, pet." I slid my fingers through his hair and gave his neck a gentle squeeze before I withdrew my touch.

He rose to his feet, too shy to make eye contact, and I handed him a pen.

"Just sign here, here, and here."

He'd read through the contracts many times over, and he'd

had access to my family lawyer—I'd offered to pay for him to have his own representation too—but he'd declined both. Naïve on his part, even though he'd told me he wasn't new to reading contracts. Even so, for all he knew, I could be some depraved bastard...

"Your trial run is over. You're mine now." I finished with my own signature and stood up. "Look at me."

He lifted his gaze to mine, and it took every bit of restraint not to kiss him. The trepidation in his eyes mingled with something much heavier. It was unmistakable, but I would be patient. His need would grow at the pace he was comfortable with.

That said, the following morning, I dressed him the way I wanted.

We were the only ones awake in our suite, and I'd locked us in the bathroom. Rather, he'd let me in once he'd showered.

I'd already gotten dressed, and I loved the image of us. Me dressed, him in only boxer briefs.

I wanted him in smaller underwear.

"Come here." I sat down on the edge of the bathtub and held his dress pants. "You'd look good in briefs."

He shuffled closer. "I don't know how to respond to that."

I chuckled quietly.

He stepped into his pants and grasped one of my shoulders.

I breathed him in, slowly pulling his pants up, my hands tracing the shape of his thighs. After seeing his upper body exposed in Santa Rosa, I'd longed for this morning. Now I could get a closer look. I could touch him.

His abs were perfectly defined the second he tensed up ever so slightly.

I ghosted my knuckles over the trail of hair leading down from his belly button.

Peyton inhaled shakily, and I wasn't sure he realized that he gripped my shoulder tighter.

His undershirt was next. I stood up, never letting him take a single step back, and pulled the white wifebeater over his head. My hands roamed his shoulders, his arms, his chest, his sides, and his abs again. Then I told him to look at me as I tucked it into his pants. With only a few inches between us, I dipped my hand into his pants, underneath the waistband of his boxer briefs, and watched his eyes flutter closed when my fingers brushed over the soft, trimmed hair around his cock.

I was going to do this. Every. Single. Morning.

While he grabbed his button-down with trembling fingers, I adjusted my cock and tugged it firmly.

Fuck.

It was going to be interesting to see who broke first, him or me.

I caught him looking at me more often.

I started coveting the glimpses of lust in his eyes more than a drug addict could crave a fix. It would be so incredibly easy to add amendments of things I wanted to do to him, but I had to hold my ground. And let him come to me.

The toughest moment was Father's Day. I didn't see it coming it all, and I was very moved by his gesture. Peyton helped Julia pick out a Father's Day card for me, and I was treated to dinner at Julia's favorite restaurant—McDonald's.

That night, I almost walked into Peyton's bedroom.

My forty-fifth birthday was next.

We were back in LA after a few shorter trips to Portland, San Jose, and San Diego.

Peyton and Julia woke me up with breakfast in bed, her crawling all over me, asking if she could blow out the candle on my English muffin, and Peyton sitting on the edge of the bed with amusement brimming in his eyes.

"Remember what we were going to do, Julia?" Peyton asked.

She perked up and cocked her head.

Peyton flashed me a slight grin and leaned closer. Closer, closer, closer. Until he brushed his lips to my cheek and whispered in my ear, "Happy birthday, Daddy."

I swallowed hard and felt like a ball of fire had just been dropped on me. It was instantly squashed by Julia landing a wet kiss to my other cheek and exclaiming, "Happ'birfday, Daddy!" but it didn't stop me from seeking out Peyton's thigh. I spread my duvet so it covered his leg, and then I dropped kisses over Julia's adorable face while I stroked the inside of Peyton's thigh, as high up as I dared to go.

"You two are amazing," I murmured. "Thank you for this."

Julia grinned goofily but then declared that this was boring and she wanted "real breakfast."

"Out there!" She pointed toward the living room. "Can't eat here, Daddy."

"I can't? Oh, I see." I chuckled and nodded in thanks when Peyton took the tray from me. "Well, let's have breakfast out there, then."

My birthday marked the end of my touring the West Coast for a while, and we headed for the airport the following evening—after we'd picked up Peyton's first bespoke suit.

He looked like I needed to fuck his brains out.

We boarded a red-eye without Mathis, because he was the

only one who wanted a layover—specifically in Denver, where he had friends. But he didn't have to be outside my building until Monday, so he could make his way home however he wanted.

Julia was as calm as ever when we flew, and she slept most of the way. But Cathryn and I knew it wouldn't last long. The time difference was too much for Julia on this route, and we prepared ourselves for an epic tantrum.

"Are we in a hurry?" Peyton blinked blearily as we deplaned.

He was starting to look like a seasoned traveler, although the neck pillow around his neck could take a hike.

"If we're lucky, she won't throw a fit until we get home," I said. I carried Julia toward baggage claim, quick strides to stay ahead, and Cathryn told us to head straight for the cabstand while she grabbed our bags.

"Daddy," Julia whined.

"I know, darling. We're almost home." I side-eyed Peyton and shook my head in amusement. "Are you going to take that off? You look ridiculous."

He scowled, then stroked the pillow lovingly. "I love my neck pillow. Julia likes it too. Don't you, sweetheart?"

"No!" she snarled.

The face Peyton made was the very definition of "Yikes."

I grinned and kissed her cheek.

"Haters," Peyton muttered. "I'll go help Cathryn instead. *Bye.*"

"Bye-bye." Julia waved.

I laughed and aimed for the exit.

It was a crisp morning in Boston, and it felt nice to be home. Summer was on its way here too, but we were in no rush.

"It's nice to be home, isn't it?" I murmured against Julia's hair. She'd buried her face against my neck and let out an occasional complaint to remind me of her presence. "I think we need McDonald's today, too. Don't you?"

"Yeah," she whined. "I'm sleepy, Daddy."

"We'll take a nap on the couch with some movies when we get home," I promised. "Then I believe your toys have missed you."

She sniffled and nodded.

When Cathryn and Peyton emerged from the airport, I told him to grab us a cab so I could relieve Cathryn of the luggage and Julia's booster seat.

"Get one for Cathryn too, please," I added.

"Yes, sir." Peyton walked over to the line for cabs.

After Cathryn had returned the cart, she let out a big sigh and smiled tiredly.

"Looking forward to a weekend off?" I asked knowingly.

She chuckled. "Yes and no. I know I'll just have to start cleaning the house. The odds of Tom having done much are not in my favor, and the boys probably need me to go restock the cupboards."

I winced in sympathy. "I've told you to use my cleaning service," I reminded. "Use my delivery service too. In fact, I'll tell Peyton to put in a request as soon as we get home. Don't argue with me."

She smashed her lips shut and gave me a frustrated look.

I smiled.

I liked to win.

A weekend in Boston turned out to be exactly what we needed. I was able to set Peyton up with his own work phone, a corporate card, and all the access codes he could need. Everything would be at the office on Monday. Julia would get some much-needed downtime, and plans were made for her to spend tomorrow with my cousin's children. Lastly, Peyton brought warmth into my home, even as he criticized my decorating style, which, frankly, wasn't mine at all. A company had done it.

"Glass table? Is this the eighties? Come on, sir."

"Jesus Christ, you're wasting this beautiful penthouse when you hide exposed brick with fucking velvet."

"You know, this is a Renaissance revival building. Maybe you've heard of something in New York called the Flatiron Building? Same style. But whereas they send tourists to the Flatiron, you hide yours. Shame on you."

"You make me wanna cry. Bronze statues?"

"I bet there are gorgeous hardwood floors under this hideous carpet."

"Thank God you left the spiral staircase alone. Judging by the rest of your additions, I'm surprised you didn't install an escalator."

"Black marble. Interesting."

The historian in Peyton was making an appearance, and he was a sassy little fucker who didn't hold back.

It was difficult to take the criticism personally, though, when I hadn't truly ever liked it myself. But the penthouse on its own suited me perfectly. I liked old buildings, and I had two floors all to myself, along with a rooftop terrace. Three bedrooms upstairs, then living room, kitchen, and office downstairs.

"First bedroom upstairs is mine, second is Julia's, the guest room after is yours," I told him. "But you might want to use my bathroom. The other one is shared between your and Julia's rooms."

"You're not going to have a go at me for so brutally annihilating your style?"

I smirked and patted his cheek on the way to the stairs. "No,

I understand you're just upset that I hurt your feelings about the neck pillow."

"I'm really not, sir!" he hollered after me.

I laughed. "So, do something about it, then. You know how to use my credit cards. Go nuts."

He huffed, glancing around the foyer. "Again, I never know if you're joking or if you're serious."

I liked it that way. It kept him on his toes.

Julia went to bed early that evening. She'd been cranky and throwing fits all day.

Now I received my reward for surviving them. The house was quiet, I'd enjoyed a long, hot shower, and it felt fantastic to be in my own bed. I'd landed stark naked on top of the duvet—everything was fresh and smelling of softener—and I had no intention of moving anytime soon.

I couldn't remember the last time I'd read for leisure.

I couldn't remember the last time I was in bed before ten either.

After adjusting my reading glasses, I placed a hand behind my head and turned the page on my tablet.

Two quiet knocks interrupted my peace, followed by, "Sir, are you awake?"

"I am," I responded. "You're free to come in, but I should warn you that I'm not wearing anything."

There was a beat of silence before he spoke again. "Um, can you cover up, then?"

I stifled a smile and turned another page. "No, I'm too comfortable."

He huffed.

I drew up one knee a bit and waited. Would he faint if he

saw the dildo in my nightstand? There was one in the bathroom too, with its own shower mount.

"I wanted to show you something, okay?" Peyton grated.

I chuckled. "Well, whatever it is, I hope I get to see it."

He wasn't anywhere near breaking point, so it couldn't be anything that resulted in the gratification I'd denied myself in the shower.

Peyton cursed. About a second later, the door opened slowly. Pleasure filled my chest, and I took a deep breath. *Good boy. Come closer.* I peered at him over the rims of my reading glasses, wondering if he was going to lift his gaze off the floor or not.

He'd showered too. His hair was still damp, and he looked comfortable in a pair of sweatpants and a T-shirt. Well. Comfortable was a relative term.

"What did you want me to see, pet?"

He swallowed hard and shifted his stare the bare minimum, and it seemed to be enough. But rather than quickly averting his gaze, he got stuck. Heat bled across his cheeks, and he just stared. *That* would cause a reaction soon if he wasn't careful. His eyes on me turned me on beyond belief.

"I, uh..." He closed the door and forced his stare back to the floor. "I haven't kneeled today, and um, I b-bought the underwear you said you thought I should have."

My God.

I took off my glasses and placed them on my nightstand with my tablet.

"Show me." It was impossible to keep the lust out of my voice completely. Soon, it would be impossible to hide it too. "Get on your knees right here next to me and show me."

He let out an unsteady breath, a sound that filled the silence, and walked over cautiously.

At the side of my bed, he gulped in some air and dropped his sweatpants, letting them pool by his feet.

I had no words. The tight, soft-looking gray cotton briefs clung to his skin so fucking perfectly. Pushing myself up on my elbows, I tilted my head and eye-fucked his delectable little ass. Then back to his front, where the fabric hugged his cock and balls. Never before had I envied fabric.

Peyton's breathing sped up as he climbed up to kneel on the mattress, and I followed his gaze to my semi-erect cock.

I tested the waters and brushed my hand up his thigh. "You have no idea how much this pleases me."

His abs clenched when I traced my fingers along the edge of his briefs.

"Do they feel good?" I asked.

He nodded quickly but didn't say anything, nor did he tear his eyes away from my cock.

Wanting to get more comfortable, I wedged another pillow behind my back so I could half sit and stay close enough to touch him. Then I reached down and wrapped my fingers around my cock, stroking it unhurriedly. He kept watching. He kept fucking watching. Christ, I needed him to break soon. I had to have him.

It brought me relief to see he was far from unaffected himself. His cock bulged under the fabric of his briefs, and I couldn't decide whether or not to touch him there. God knew I wanted to.

"Do you enjoy kneeling for me?"

"Yes, sir," he exhaled.

I let out a quiet groan and stroked myself a little harder.

He sucked in a breath.

"Such a beautiful little boy." I couldn't help myself. I slid my hand to his ass and kneaded one of the cheeks firmly, and the whimper that escaped him almost did me in. His cock was straining in his briefs at that point, and I spied the smallest of wet spots darkening the gray fabric. It made my mouth water. "You're going to watch me come, aren't you?"

He nodded jerkily and balled his hands into fists along his sides.

"Very soon," I promised. "All mine..." I groped at his ass, squeezing it until I could see redness appearing in blotchy prints after my thumb. "I own you. Don't I, Peyton?"

"Yes, sir," he moaned.

"That's a good boy." The urgency built up rapidly, and I slipped my hand underneath his briefs. "Say, 'You own me, sir.'"

"You own me, sir," he gasped.

I groaned loudly, fisting my cock tightly, stroking it faster and faster, and felt the pleasure pooling lower and lower. "Say, 'You own me, Daddy.'"

His breathing stuttered, and he quickly cupped his cock, squeezing it. "You own me, Daddy."

"Don't touch yourself," I grunted and pushed away his hand. "*Fuck*, boy. I'm gonna come. Oh God, Peyton. Daddy's coming." I succumbed to the euphoria, and it ripped through me with a force that would've floored me if I hadn't been in bed. Ropes of come splashed against my abdomen, flooding the air with the scent of sex.

God-fucking-damn.

There was no word to describe how much I'd needed that.

I swallowed dryly and collapsed against the mattress.

"Sir," Peyton gritted. "M-may I be excused?"

I frowned and blinked, squinting up at him, and worry was the first thing that shot up my spine. Until I got a proper look at him. He was practically shaking with need. The wet spot in his briefs had grown larger, and I'd never seen him strung so tight.

He needed to get off. But he wasn't bold enough to ask me to help him. Or maybe he wasn't ready yet.

"If you assure me that everything's all right," I told him seriously, still catching my breath.

He nodded furiously and scrambled off the bed. "Everything is fine, sir, I promise. I promise, I promise. I just gotta go. Oh my God." He tumbled for the door and fled the scene.

CHAPTER 7.

I was up with the sun the next morning. I'd slept well, but Peyton had remained on the fringes of my conscience. I wanted to make sure he was okay.

I'd heard him upstairs around seven, about the same time I tried my hand at making a frittata. Peyton had mentioned it being one of his favorites. I didn't know what the fuck I was doing, but...I was even using tomatoes in his half.

Julia wasn't fond of eggs, though I suspected she would try it —unless I burned it. She tended to try anything Peyton liked.

It was sweet.

I cocked my head toward the stairs when I heard the unmistakable sound of Julia's less than graceful stumble. She said something, and Peyton responded.

While waiting for the frittata to be done, I set the table in the dining area—that supposedly belonged in the eighties.

It did look kind of awful.

To be honest, I'd never given it much thought. My home was a place to sleep, a place to ensure Julia's well-being. She'd been my sole focus for almost three years. Balancing work and my daughter had been my only task.

I wasn't looking forward to the anniversary of Sandra's death. Or Mona's, for that matter.

"Daddy, open de gate, pwlease!"

"It's okay. I've got her," Peyton said.

Perfect timing. I heard the gate to the stairs open and close, and the frittata looked ready.

"Daddy say babypwoofing is impowtant, but I'm a big girl now," Julia told Peyton seriously.

I grinned to myself and carried the last of it to the table.

"I think we listen to him on this one, sweetheart," Peyton chuckled. "Something smells awesome, doesn't it?"

"Maybe." She was undecided.

Shit, I'd forgotten our coffee. And it reminded me that I didn't know how Peyton preferred his.

I found myself wanting to know things like that, something I hadn't cared about in the past.

"G'mornin', Daddy!" Julia exclaimed as they rounded the corner. She was adorable in her rumpled, pajama-clad morning glory.

I smiled at her. Her pronunciation was getting better with each day. "Good morning, you two."

Peyton was dressed casually like me, in jeans and a tee. Beautiful and striking as ever, but I wasn't going to waste a minute to get to the bottom of his somewhat guarded smile. It was too polite. Too business.

"Peyton, help me with something in the kitchen, please," I said, heading that way.

"Uh-oh. Do you think I'm in trouble?" Peyton joked, setting Julia down on the floor.

She giggled. "Oops?"

I waited by the coffeemaker, leaning back against the counter. Black marble. Peyton had made a face and called it "Interesting."

As Peyton trailed in, appearing uncertain, I straightened and felt my chest constrict uncomfortably.

"Did I go too far last night?" I asked.

He shook his head but averted his gaze to the floor. "No, sir."

"It's not easy to believe you when you won't look at me." Fuck, I'd crossed a line.

"I swear you didn't." He adjusted one of the magnets on the fridge. "It was intense. I couldn't deal at the end. I...I don't know how to explain it."

"You're going to have to do your best to try," I told him, feeling queasy all of a sudden. "I won't do it again. I'm very sorry if—"

"No!" He rushed out the word and took a couple steps closer. "Please don't. I don't know what happened. I've never felt anything like it before."

I waited. Hopeful but unsatisfied. Christ, he was worrying me. I should've communicated better; that was for certain.

"Please don't stop," he whispered. Taking another couple steps brought him within a foot of me, and he lifted his gaze to a spot near my shoulder. "Tell me what you need."

Honestly? "Right now? I need a damn hug, but I'm—" That was all I got out before he closed the distance and hugged my middle. I blew out a heavy breath and hugged him to me. "Tell me what *you* need."

"This."

I kissed his temple and cupped the back of his head, my other hand roaming his shoulder blades and spine. "Promise me."

"I promise." He breathed in deeply and rested his forehead against my collarbone.

Relief flowed through me. "Were you truly all right last night?"

He chuckled awkwardly. "Uh, yeah. I left because I was

literally a second away from coming. Without touching—you know."

A slow grin took over, and I pressed another kiss to his hair. "Did you?"

"I'm not telling you," he insisted. "Just...don't stop, okay? You push me so far outside of my comfort zone, it's not even funny, and it's...it's a rush. So, don't stop. You promised me a journey."

I did, didn't I?

Very well, then.

On Tuesday, after one commercial flight and a quick drive, we arrived at Miami Executive, where our private jet for the next few weeks was fueled and ready for our departure.

"This is fucking nuts," Peyton mumbled.

Mathis loaded our luggage onto a cart to get it through a quick scan, while the rest of us moved ahead.

"Wha's fuckin' nuts?" Julia asked curiously.

I chuckled and carried her through security, where I showed an agent our passports.

"We don't have to stand in line," Peyton responded in wonder. "A guy could get used to this."

It was certainly comfortable.

He was weirdly cute when he had to show his passport for the first time. He tried to contain his grin when he handed it over to the operator, but his eyes said it all. *Look at me, I'm going places. I have my own passport.* The response from the agent was underwhelming, not that Peyton cared.

Once we were through, we walked straight out to the plane.

"To the beeeeeach," Julia sang, waving her arms.

"My adorable girl." I kissed her cheek and walked up the

steps where one of the two flight attendants greeted us with a warm smile.

There were six seats, plus a private area in the back with an additional three seats. If I remembered correctly, two of those chairs in the back made a couch, and it would be Julia's downtime place.

Cathryn and Julia sat across from each other on one side of the aisle, and Peyton dutifully took his seat across from me on the other side.

Mathis joined us and greeted the pilots once our luggage was loaded onto the aircraft.

As one of the flight attendants asked Cathryn if she wanted a drink, Peyton leaned forward and spoke for only me to hear.

"Should you perhaps punish me for being a bad influence on Julia's vocabulary?"

Well, well.

My boy was getting bolder.

"I'm sorry to disappoint you," I said, amused, "but Julia cursed long before you entered the picture. Her daddy's language isn't the cleanest either." Although, I could admit I'd at least tried to pretend to care before. I'd made it clear that she wasn't *supposed* to curse. "Lastly"—it was my turn to lean forward and lower my voice—"you don't have to worry your pretty little head about my plans for you."

"Hmpf."

"My God." I set down the report on the table between us and scrubbed at my eyes. "I'm already seeing numbers in my dreams."

I was sick of them.

Peyton glanced up from his phone. "Shouldn't you wear your glasses?"

"I *should*..." I never traveled with them. I hadn't gotten into the habit of wearing them for work yet. I got them last year, after I kept getting headaches. "I need a break. That's what I need." After clearing the table, I flipped it down below the window again. I'd been looking forward to a view of Peyton across from me, but then we'd been served a light meal, and when the table was up, I'd figured I could get some work done too. No more, though. "You can part your legs for me a bit more."

"What?"

I gave him a pointed look. "Do I need to repeat myself every time I have a demand?"

He flicked a nervous glance at the empty seats around us. Well, Mathis was asleep in the last row, and Cathryn and Julia were watching a movie in the back.

"No, sir." Peyton cleared his throat and shifted in his seat to give me a proper manspread. He wore his dark navy suit today, and it fit him perfectly. White shirt, mercury tie.

I inhaled deeply and got comfortable in my seat, resting one ankle over my knee.

"I love dressing you," I admitted. "Even Daddy wants to play with dolls every now and then."

"Christ," Peyton whispered under his breath.

I wanted to press my face against the swell of his crotch.

The flight attendant came to take another drink order, and I handed over the empty glass from the shallow cupholder in my armrest.

"Same, thank you. Whiskey, neat."

"One for me too, please." Peyton extended his glass as well. "Thank you."

I absolutely loved that he was all man. He could be deliciously boyish at times, and so thoroughly lure out the decadent beast in me, but he was, first and foremost, a young man seeking to carve out his place in the world. He drank whiskey from time to time, sometimes wine, beer, and gin and tonic, even an old-fashioned once. I'd learned he took his coffee black. He was well-mannered, social, and never shied away from taking care of others. Naturally, his sister and mother, primarily, but I wasn't blind to his fondness for my daughter. Peyton was wonderful with her, and I believed it was partly because he actually liked her.

He was also intelligent and educated, neither of which he showcased as if he had something to brag about. Instead, he waited for people to listen to him. He had patience, I'd discovered. Much more than I did. He listened before he spoke.

My hunger for knowing more about him kept growing.

I only got glimpses here and there. This was his first time seeing our country, and he was introspective enough that he kept his reactions mostly to himself. I'd seen his eyes light up at the sight of Boston Harbor, though he hadn't said anything. He'd gazed in awe at the Golden Gate when we'd crossed it during our trip to San Francisco, and he'd people watched with enthusiasm in Santa Monica.

I wanted to get into his head.

"Where did your interest in history come from?" I asked.

He flashed a curious look at the change of topic, but he didn't hesitate to answer. "My grandmother. Well, her whole family. She was the youngest and had six brothers who all fought in World War II. She saved their journals and letters and gave them to me."

I was a bit of a history lover myself, and there was no dousing the spark of interest. "Personal stories always fascinated me the most."

"I know." His eyes gave off a warm glow of mirth and fondness. "I may have checked out your library."

I chuckled. If only I had a library of my own. What I did have were floor-to-ceiling shelves in the living room, one unit reserved for military history.

"Did your grandmother's brothers make it back?"

He shook his head. "Only two of them survived the war. One drank himself to death a few years after. But Jefferson, the second youngest, died of old age when I was fourteen. His stories were my drug."

I could imagine. My family was part English and part French, and they moved to the US right after the war. I was surrounded by veterans growing up. "An uncle of my father's wrote a book about our family members who fought in the war. I must've read it a dozen times before I graduated high school."

Peyton blushed a little for some reason. "It's possible I found it. I reacted to the author's last name—Delamare. It's also possible it's in my room now."

I grinned. It made me happy that he was curious about my family too.

"Then I don't have to tell you any stories," I said. "I'll listen to yours instead. Did your grandmother's brothers fight in Europe or in the Pacific Theater?"

"Mostly the latter," he answered. "One of them went to Italy, but the others were scattered around the Pacific. Jefferson was a Marine at Iwo Jima. The two eldest were there too, but they were in the Navy, so they didn't go ashore."

Peyton needed little to no prompting to share tales of his family members, and he was an amazing storyteller. He spoke animatedly about one of the brothers in particular, who'd been a Navy pilot. He even made me forget where I was.

Then he mentioned, just in passing, something that brought me back to the present.

His grandmother had died when Peyton was sixteen. Two

years before his sister was born. He'd truly had no one else once his sister was in his care.

Goddammit, I was getting emotionally attached.

"Sir, wake up."

I was almost there anyway... Since Cathryn had already taken Julia to the beach, I thought I'd get some extra rest.

"Sir."

"Yes, yes." I groaned and stretched out, then rolled onto my back and dragged a hand over my face. "What is it?"

Peyton stood in the doorway with clothes draped over his arm. "We're in paradise, and I'm wondering how strict you are about clothes in eighty-five-degree heat."

I chuckled drowsily and dragged myself up to lean back against the headboard.

It'd been dark when we'd arrived at our resort here in Martinique last night; it was understandable that Peyton wanted to go explore. But we had a meeting at eleven, so work came first.

"I'm quite generous, actually," I yawned. "You don't have to wear a tie."

He blinked. "You call that generous, sir?"

"I do." I smiled and patted the spot next to me. "Let's see what you're wearing today." I shifted my legs off the mattress, and my feet landed on the granite floor tiles. Everything in the resort was new, after a hurricane passed straight through a couple years ago. The main building had been restored, but the bungalows, the clubhouse, the pool area with two restaurants and three bars, and the activity center had to be rebuilt from the foundations.

"I ate out on the terrace in just my trunks, and I got sweaty," he said.

"So, you'll have a refreshing shower later, in other words," I replied. "I'm having the maid service pick up a few of my suits for dry-cleaning today. You should have some items you need washed too, yes?"

"Yes, sir." He tossed his gray suit pants, socks, and a light blue shirt on the bed. "Are those okay?"

"Definitely. Just make sure you wear your suit jacket too." I leaned forward and grazed my nose along his abs. *Mmm.* He smelled amazing. He must've showered already too. Pushing away the sheets pooling around my middle, I stood up and wasn't too surprised when Peyton cursed.

"Do you always sleep naked?"

"Yes. You should try it." I hooked two fingers into the waistband of his trunks. How disappointing. He wore briefs under them. "Take these off." Next, I moved to stand behind him when he bent over. I grabbed him by his hips, hard, and pressed my cock against his ass.

That got me a lovely reaction. He gasped and almost fell forward.

"Jesus," he breathed.

"I'll say." I released him slowly and kneaded his perfect ass cheeks. Today was the day I was going to see him without underwear, I decided. "You're making your boss hard, Peyton."

"I'm sorry?" he squeaked. Fucking squeaked. How I wanted to take advantage of his embarrassment. It was so goddamn sexy.

As he straightened up, pants in his hands, he stood there and didn't know what to do. The trembling was back, and I soaked it up. He'd sunk back into that vulnerable state that drove me *fucking* wild.

"Put on your pants, my pretty doll," I murmured in his ear. "Daddy's going to play with you so much during this trip."

He made a low *hnngh* sound, as if he was swallowing a moan.

A plan formed in my head while I traced a finger in the crease between his ass cheeks. The briefs wouldn't be in the way next time I touched him there. But first, I was going to offer a false sense of security. As per our agreement, I was to apply sunscreen to him while we were in the Caribbean, and it would be so fun to give him a rug to stand on before I ripped it away. For example, by using the sunscreen spray I used for myself. A couple times, perhaps. I'd barely touch him.

How would that compare to what he anticipated? He'd seen me pack the sunscreen lotion at home already. He knew it was coming.

He just didn't know when.

"Fuck," I muttered and peered down. "Now you made me all hard."

Peyton failed to be discreet. He looked behind him quickly while he zipped up his pants.

"You can get dressed while I shower instead. Drop your pants again." I went over to my closet and grabbed my second toiletry kit. "Come with me to the bathroom for a minute."

That seemed to spike his nerves, and he followed me with anxiousness rolling off his shoulders. "Wh-what're you gonna do to me?"

I hid my smirk. Truth be told, with the number of fantasies I'd buried over the years, combined with how new to this Peyton was, it didn't take more than a fraction of a second to pick something that would push him out of his comfort zone, as he'd called it himself. And it was exactly where I wanted him.

"I'm not going to do anything to you." I sent him a frown of confusion, as if I found his question odd. "I just thought you could help me shave."

"O-oh," he stuttered.

Once in the bathroom, I set my toiletry kit next to my other one. "I told you to take off your pants again," I reminded.

"Fuck. Yes, sir. Sorry, sir."

I made sure to lock the door before I walked back to the counter again. Over the sink, I washed my face and took out my razor and shaving gel. By then, Peyton was standing there in just his briefs. They were white today. I preferred gray, only because they stained easier.

"Hop up here." I patted the counter next to the sink. "I trust you know how to shave."

"Yes, sir, but I've never done it to someone else," he replied hesitantly. "I don't want to hurt you."

"That's sweet, little one," I murmured and touched his cheek, "but I'm not worried."

Considering what I was about to do, it would be weird if I didn't get nicked once or twice.

I watched him get into position and soak a hand towel in warm water, and he left the water running. In the meantime, I rubbed my cock absently, certain it wouldn't take many seconds before I was rock solid again.

The faint splash of pink over his cheeks let me know he kept me in his periphery.

When he was ready, I moved closer and slipped my hands around his knees, to the undersides of them, and parted his legs enough for me to step between. Goose bumps rose across his shoulders and chest. His nipples constricted.

"Shave me, pet."

He took a breath and nodded, reaching for the shaving gel.

I stepped even closer.

It was perfect. I was going to watch his face. Watch his reactions to my touches.

Peyton seemed to struggle with putting all his focus on his task. He tried to concentrate. With a smooth and gentle hand, he applied the gel over my jaw, my cheeks, my chin, and a couple inches down my neck. I enjoyed the touch more than I'd anticipated. Having his hands on me was a gift.

Even so, he couldn't stop his reactions to what I did. When I rubbed his thighs, dangerously close to his crotch, he swallowed hard and squirmed. When I slid my hands up his abs, he shivered. When I reached his chest, he almost closed his eyes.

I plucked at his nipples, twisting them carefully to test his threshold.

"Your stubble grows fast," he murmured breathily. "It's so raspy."

"Mm. I've heard it feels nice to have between your legs."

"Oh." He swallowed, and a crease formed between his brows. Maybe he was concentrating again. It was time to use the razor, and he did the first pass over my jaw very slowly. "Other men have told you that," he stated quietly. "Others you've been with."

My mouth twitched.

Was that jealousy I was hearing? It couldn't be.

"Other assistants?" he asked.

"No." I pinched his nipple a little harder and grasped my cock with my free hand. "We have a no-fraternization policy at Westwater, and once upon a time, I actually took it seriously."

That appeared to lighten the tension. Mirth seeped into his eyes. "Did you really?"

"Mm. I'd go so far as to say I've never been tempted before."

"I see." The sweet boy liked hearing that. "Then you met me?"

I chuckled. "Then I met you." It warmed my heart to

witness his pleasure, but the dominant bastard in me wanted to tone down the smugness. So, I closed the distance between us and locked his feet around my ass. "Keep them there while Daddy rubs his cock all over your pretty underwear."

That earned me the first nick along the edge of my jaw, and the sweetest part was that Peyton became genuinely distraught. He apologized over and over for being startled, and he cleaned the spot with a corner of the damp towel.

"That's enough, pet. I'm *fine*. Get back to shaving me." I emphasized just how "injured" I was by pressing my cock against his semisoft bulge and covering myself with my hands. God, that felt good. It wasn't a wet, warm, tight hole, but it was his cock against mine.

I instantly noticed how smooth his sac was, even through the fabric of his briefs. Either he'd shaved his balls very recently, or he barely had any hair on them in the first place.

Peyton sank his teeth into his bottom lip and slid the razor over my cheek.

"It probably wouldn't be nice of me if I spoiled your underwear, would it?" I peered down as much as I could without interrupting what he was doing, and I rubbed the head of my cock along the length of his. "It's hard to resist, though," I murmured. "I love groping you. I love seeing how embarrassed you get." I teased the tips of two fingers along the seam of the fabric and tested the elasticity. Oh, that would work. The underwear had plenty of give, despite being so snug. "I think Daddy's cock wants in here." I dipped my fingers underneath and scratched his trimmed hair. "What do you say, little boy? Should we let it?"

He made a soft, needy sound that went straight to my cock. "If you want, sir."

"I want. Spread your legs as if you're a desperate little slut." I helped him, because I couldn't fucking wait.

As his chest started heaving, I unleashed my need and manhandled him. I grabbed at his thighs, pressing myself as close as I could. The urgency blasted within, and I barely registered the sound of the razor clanking into the sink. Fuck, I had to feel him. Now. Right fucking now. I lifted his underwear, and I forced my cock toward his. Skin on skin. *Fuck, fuck, fuck.* That was it. I trapped my cock under his and pressed a hand over his swelling bulge, and then I fucked the tight gap.

"Fuck," I groaned. I rubbed the underside of his cock; its head pointed toward his abs, and the wet spot forming at the tip caused the same reaction in me as last time. My mouth watered. I wanted to taste him soon. I wanted to feel his cock in my throat, in my ass, in my hands.

Peyton whimpered and dug his fingernails into my biceps.

"Look what you're making me do," I said, breathing heavily. "I can't fucking control myself around you. Here—hold here." I placed his hand over his cock. "Press down so you make it tight for Daddy."

"Yes, Daddy," he gasped.

I gnashed my teeth and hooked an arm under his knee. Then I almost folded him in half and fucked him up against the counter. Over and over, I pushed my erection into the space between his cock and the smooth flesh above it. His soft hairs scratched my skin with every thrust, and my pre-come turned the makeshift hole warm and slick.

I gripped the back of his neck and nipped at his jaw. "We're both gonna come in your underwear, Peyton," I whispered. "We're gonna make such a fucking mess out of you."

"Oh fuck!" He threw his head back, the sexiest goddamn sight, and rubbed furiously at his cock.

It sent vibrations up my shaft, and I fucked him harder, faster, pushing my cock through the crease with punishing thrusts.

"You'll look so good in Daddy's come." I licked a bead of perspiration that trickled down his neck, until I reached his earlobe. I sucked it into my mouth. "It's time, baby. Come for Daddy. Soak my cock. Flood your underwear."

Mere seconds later, he went rigid and let out a loud moan.

Warm come pulsed through the fabric, making his fingers glisten, and it trickled down to my cock too. As the scent of him reached my nostrils, I let go. Whether I wanted to or not. The bliss took over. I pushed against him once more, gliding through his orgasm with ease, and came.

"Oh my God," he whimpered. "Oh my *God*."

I groaned and bit into his shoulder.

Jesus Christ, what was this man doing to me?

This whole "I'm not going to budge an inch" bit wasn't working out too well.

CHAPTER
8.

I remember when you asked me about my experience with BDSM.

The truth is, I'd read a blog entry about a Daddy Dominant and his Little Girl just the night before that'd hit so close to home, I'd almost started weeping. Back then, you were waking up parts of me I hadn't even known were dormant in me.

It was right around here you became my world. I clung to everything you said.

That's never going to change, Edward.

"Are you looking, Daddy?" Julia yelled, adjusting her floaties.

"Of course I am, my love." I lowered my newspaper and watched as she darted into the pool where Peyton was waiting to catch her.

I grinned when my girl surfaced with a victory shout.

"That was fantastic," Peyton praised her.

"Did you see, Daddy?" she called.

I chuckled. "I saw every second of it. You're doing so great."

"Yeah," she laughed. "Chase me, Peyton."

"Okay, I'm gonna chase ya."

I smiled and shook my head at her antics. She swam about as gracefully as a dog with those floaties around her arms, but damn, she belonged in the water. She was fearless—sometimes too fearless. When I was in the pool with her, I let her get rid of the floaties, and she simply counted on me always being there to hold her up. She could throw herself in any direction without warning.

"Damn, we needed this weekend." Cathryn stretched out on the lounger next to mine. If I were to venture a guess, she didn't miss her family right this second.

"Indeed." I hummed, returning to my paper.

Our first two weeks in the Caribbean had been hectic, and we'd covered Martinique, Montserrat, St. Croix, St. Thomas, the Dominican Republic, and Aruba so far. Yesterday, we arrived here in Jamaica for a much-needed break.

Peyton had received a reality check and no longer thought my job was glamorous "100% of the time." We'd had back-to-back meetings with staff, managers, and local ad agencies that drained us to the point where we collapsed at the end of the day and didn't care about dinner. Water was the constant requirement. Frequent showers and ice-cold water to drink.

In the end, I chose to focus on my obsession with Peyton. He was getting...antsy. I still managed to make him blush with the occasional touch or something I said, but I hadn't made any new advances since our rendezvous in Martinique.

The first time I sprayed sunscreen on him, I thought I was going to lose it. His expression had been priceless. And I *definitely* hadn't missed the disappointment on his face. The sweet boy had expected more groping.

He needn't worry. We were staying in Jamaica for four days,

and I only had three work commitments. Tomorrow, I was taking him—and only him—to a private beach.

If he thought my current swimwear "put everything on display," wait till I wasn't wearing any at all.

I didn't know what was wrong with the trunks I had on, to be honest. They were black, comfortable, and had the exact same cut as regular boxer briefs. Hell, Cathryn's husband wore identical trunks. She was the one who sent me the link to them.

"Daddy!" Julia hollered. "Come swim wid us!"

I probably should. It was getting hot, and I wasn't sure if it was sunscreen or sweat that made my chest hair sparkle like a drag queen at this point.

I got up from my lounger with a grunt and tossed my shades on my towel.

"Yay, floaties off!" she cheered.

I laughed softly and sat down on the edge of the pool. The water felt cold, so it was a good idea to cool down. I'd been in the sun since breakfast. As I lowered myself into the water, cursing at the temperature, Julia threw off her floaties and hurled herself from Peyton's embrace. It was a good thing he fished her out of the water.

"You're a little nut, darling," I told her. "You can't swim yet."

"Yuh-huh!" she argued and spluttered.

I dove under the surface, only to emerge when she was within reach. Slipping my hands under her armpits, I pulled her to me and peppered her face with kisses.

She giggled madly and pushed my cheeks together.

"Am I cute now?" I asked, puckering my lips.

She found me hilarious enough to give me a big smooch. "Daddies can't be cute."

"Says who?" I laughed.

She shrugged. "I dunno."

"I think some daddies can be cute," Peyton said and swam around us in a circle. "Especially your daddy."

I puffed out my chest and smirked smugly. "Hear that, Julia?"

"Really?" She scrunched her nose and hooked her arm around my neck. "You think my daddy's cute?"

Peyton nodded, his lips near the surface of the water, and swam up to us. To my surprise, he stroked his hand along my lower back while he booped Julia on the nose.

She gigglesnorted and batted away his hand.

Peyton's hand on my back stayed, though.

Tomorrow couldn't come fast enough.

All of us had breakfast together on the terrace of our bungalow the following morning, including Mathis, who was tagging along with the girls on an excursion today. Most of our island resorts in the Caribbean provided luxury for scuba divers, golfers, spa-goers, and wealthy sport fishing enthusiasts, so our properties were off the beaten path and about a twenty-minute drive to the nearest town or village. And today, Cathryn wanted to go shopping.

I felt better knowing Mathis would be there as security.

Peyton was under the impression that we had a work commitment before our brief vacation could resume, so he wished Julia a great time and expressed that he was a little jealous he couldn't come with.

He'd be more than a little jealous in a while, but it would pass—if he agreed to my next request.

"Okay, so where are we off to?" he asked. "I'm supposed to let you know where you gotta be, not the other way around."

"As my assistant, certainly. But today you're just my pretty property." I finished my coffee and stood up. "Let's get some sunscreen on you, and then we'll head out."

"All right," he responded, confused, and followed me inside. Toward the bathroom.

I'd already changed into cargo shorts and a tee, so I was ready to go. Hell, I'd been ready since one of the hotel staff had delivered the golf cart out front earlier. At nine, I'd received confirmation that everything was ready on the private beach.

It belonged to the resort and was only a five-minute ride away from here.

"Isn't it smarter to use the spray outside?" he asked.

Probably, but I wasn't using the spray this time.

"I think it's wise that you don't question my decisions, pet. Arms out and close your eyes."

He sighed and positioned himself in front of the mirror.

I smiled, grabbing the lotion from one of my kits. It pleased me to see him so relaxed. He thought he was safe and protected here.

He put his trunks on first thing in the morning, and he wore them without a shirt until work called. But today, he'd wear nothing, so I had to make sure he wouldn't get sunburned anywhere.

Even where the sun didn't shine, I mused to myself.

After pouring a generous amount into my hand, I coated my fingers and eased them out over Peyton's shoulders. He jumped at the contact, and his eyes flashed open. They met mine in the mirror.

"Don't disobey me, Peyton."

He exhaled and screwed them shut again.

I took my time, always loving having my hands on him. I traced the ridges of his muscles. I rubbed his flesh. I wondered... about his experience with men in the past. I didn't believe he was completely inexperienced, though I suspected dominance and submission was new. Perhaps he'd read about it—or watched porn with it.

Pressing a kiss to the back of his neck, I reached around him and massaged the lotion into his chest. "Have you had boyfriends before, little one?"

He twitched slightly. "Sort of. More like I've dated men casually. A little."

A little.

"Girlfriends?" I guessed.

"Yes, sir." That was a more assertive response. Then he hesitated a bit before adding, "I'm more drawn to men, but it's been difficult. I haven't really felt...compatible."

I applied more lotion. "Explain."

He lowered his arms slowly, waiting for me to protest, but it was all right. "I like what you're doing," he confessed. "I love to please you."

I hummed and pressed my lips to his neck again. "You've been a good boy to me."

He shuddered as I rubbed my hands over his abs. "You're so fucking sexy," he whispered. Pleasure coursed through me to hear that, more than I could've expected. "I never know what you're going to do. You're shameless, confident, so goddamn masculine. You own the world."

Heavens, where was this coming from?

"I can follow you," he went on quietly. I wondered if it was easier for him to communicate when his eyes were closed. It appeared that way. "I don't have to top."

Hmm. "Have you been a top with previous lovers?"

He nodded. "I like it, but...mentally, it's... I don't know how to explain."

I could guess, though, and I almost wished I would be wrong. Because he couldn't be *that* perfect. Christ, I'd lose my heart to him if he turned out to be the missing puzzle piece I'd longed for even when I was surrounded by kinksters.

"Separate the mind from the body, dear." I dipped a lotion-coated hand into his trunks and cupped his cock.

He gasped. "Oh my God."

I groped him like I wanted to, tugging on his cock and balls until he was pressing himself against me.

"Focus, little boy," I chided. "Mentally, you're submissive, but you have physical urges as both a top and a bottom—is that what you're saying?"

"Yes," he whimpered. "Fuck—I think so. I haven't bottomed."

Possessiveness roared ahead, and I had to gnash my teeth to restrain myself. Somewhat. Not completely. I withdrew my hand from his groin and poured more lotion, and then I slipped my hand down to his ass instead. I had to feel him a bit.

I didn't give him any warning. I slid my fingers between his cheeks and reached his opening. A tight, soft, untouched little opening.

Peyton sucked in a stuttered breath and smacked his hands onto the counter, his fingers trying fruitlessly to dig into the marble surface.

"You're telling me this is a virgin little bottom, Peyton?" I pushed the tip of my index finger inside him, and he groaned and nodded. "Christ. How's Daddy gonna stay away now? This makes me want to visit your room in the middle of the night and take you in your sleep."

The answer was, Daddy *wouldn't* stay away. But I'd practice patience a short while longer.

Peyton all but collapsed over the counter when I withdrew from him and declared he was ready for a day in the sun.

"Are you just g-gonna leave me l-like this?" he stammered incredulously.

"Of course not. I'm gonna bring you with me. Let's go."

Peyton was...*cranky*. It was endearing, funny, and very Julia-like.

It was as if he were reverting mentally, a heady idea that drove me insane with desire. It was evidence. Evidence that he felt relaxed enough, that he trusted me enough, to let go of social constructs and boundaries.

I'd never gone beyond age play when I was active in BDSM, though I'd always had a soft spot for DD/lb. A dear friend of mine was a Daddy Dom, and it was because of him and his Little Boy I found it a lovely fetish. Perhaps with Peyton, I'd get a taste of it for myself. We had the chemistry, in my opinion.

Who knew. Maybe one day.

"Will you stop moping, boy?" I pulled him to me and draped an arm around his shoulders. "It's a gorgeous day, we don't have any work, and it's just you and me." Using my free hand, I steered the golf cart alongside the expansive hills and bunkers that made up the resort's golf course.

The other side of the path was all jungle, and past that, sandy white beaches and turquoise water.

"I'm not moping," he argued. "I'm demonstrating how I feel when you leave me hanging all the time."

I let out a laugh and twisted his nipple.

"Ow!" He pushed away my hand, and yet, he shifted closer and leaned against my side. "Where are we going anyway?"

"Someplace private." I pressed a kiss to the side of his head.

We'd reached the end of the golf course, and I turned right. There was a staffed gate, and a woman let us through. After that, it was a short drive straight through the jungle.

I rubbed Peyton's chest, my fingers returning to his nipples.

I liked to play with them. They constricted when I came near, and he broke out in goose flesh so easily.

"Oh, wow." Peyton gazed up ahead, where a strip of white and a patch of blue parted the jungle. "We're going to a beach?"

"Mmhmm."

It was a small cove that was part of a bigger lagoon. The beach itself was no larger than some thirty or forty feet, and the crystal-clear water was cradled by cliffs that were anything but pleasant to walk on. It was possible I'd ventured up on one last time I was here.

Julia didn't remember it. She'd been too young, but it was comfortable to take her to this specific beach because of the netted barrier between the bases of the outer cliffs. I already had her to worry about; no need to add sharks, jellyfish, and stingrays.

Peyton and I emerged from the jungle and entered heaven on earth.

Everything had been taken care of. The cabana was to the right, with billowing white fabrics hanging down the sides. Not too far away was the tiniest of bungalows; it only held a bathroom and a supply closet. A shower with running fresh-water stood right outside of it. And lastly, a barbecue area that'd been prepared for us. I had a note from the staff with instructions on where to find everything from the icebox to the barbecue tongs.

I had reason to believe some of the staff thought I was daft.

"Holy shit," Peyton breathed. He was out of the golf cart in a second and just as quick to pull out his phone. "I'm gonna take a hundred photos of this place."

I gave myself a mental pat on the back. He hadn't reacted as audibly to the Golden Gate or Boston Harbor.

"We're really gonna be here all day?" he asked in wonder.

"If you want." I smiled and grabbed the bag and the cooler

I'd packed. "I told Cathryn and Mathis we'd meet them for drinks at the hotel around nine. That's all."

I couldn't wait to get out of my clothes, so I carried our things to the cabana, where a king-size bed waited for us. Other than the mattress being firmer than a regular bed, it had the same sheets and pillows as found in the rest of the resort.

"Do you know what I would've been doing now if I hadn't met you?" Peyton jogged after me. "*Not this.*"

I chuckled and pulled my tee over my head.

"I'm very grateful, you know." He stepped closer and brushed a hand along my side. "You're giving me the adventure of a lifetime."

I smiled despite the fact that his words didn't leave me with a warm and fuzzy feeling. It was a reminder I needed, perhaps. This was an adventure for him. A journey. A big experience. And I was only one part of it.

"I like doing things for you." I palmed his cheek and pressed a light kiss to his forehead. "You've made my life so much easier, Peyton."

He offered a wobbly smile before he took a step back. "You've made, um, some things harder for me."

I broke into a full-fledged grin and almost kissed him right then and there. He was utterly charming and funny, and I...I was in trouble. Peyton turned the promises I'd made to myself into guidelines with wiggle room, and if I was using his body to live out my fantasies, that wiggle room was more vast than the ocean. An adventure, that was what I was. I could keep giving him that for as long as he was with me. It should be enough.

Kissing him now would blur things further. I *wanted* to kiss him. It hadn't been my intention to hold off more than...well, I'd been hoping he would come to me. I'd been planning—foolishly—that if I drove him to the brink of desperation, he'd throw himself at me.

Christ. Sandra used to call me a hopeless romantic, something I'd never hesitated to scoff at and refute.

In retrospect, maybe she'd been right.

While Peyton threw off his T-shirt and announced he was running into the water, I stayed back a minute to get my wits about me again. We were having an incredible time together; there was no reason that had to stop. Hopefully, we could enjoy this year to the fullest, *with* kisses—as soon as I'd screwed my head on right again. Wet, hungry, passionate kisses and countless nights of hard, sweaty fucking.

I blew out a breath, feeling a bit better.

Time to show that young man how one properly experienced a private beach.

After stripping off my clothes, I sprayed myself down with some sunscreen and then made my way to the water. The sun felt good on my body, and I rubbed the sunscreen droplets into my skin.

"You have no shame whatsoever, do you?" Peyton called from the water.

"Should I?" I asked.

He shook his head and watched me move toward him. "You're probably the hottest man I've ever met, but I can't function when you gotta be naked all the fucking time."

Oh, that ego boost. I needed it badly.

When the water was deep enough, I dove under the surface and washed away the discomfort from earlier. The water wasn't as salty in the lagoon, making it possible for me to open my eyes underwater and resurface right where Peyton stood in the perfectly white sand. Which reminded me, I'd brought snorkeling masks for later. The narrow reef along the western cliff was beautiful. There were plenty of colorful fish and the occasional starfish.

I pulled Peyton close to me and kissed his neck. "You make an old man feel young again."

"Old," he snorted.

I smirked. "Seasoned."

I'd expected some humor in return. Instead, he circled me and roamed his hands over my back.

"Distinguished," he murmured. "I love the silver right here." He pecked my temple. "And your chest..." He slipped his hands to my front and brushed his fingers through my chest hair. "Don't get me started on your thighs. Next to you, I feel like I have chicken legs."

"Don't be ridiculous." I hauled him to my front again and wrapped his legs around my hips. "Actually—" I untangled us and tugged at his trunks. "It's time to take these off, pet. You've denied me for too long."

He widened his eyes. "*I've* denied *you*? You've acted like a fucking cocktease!"

"Easy." I hitched a brow in warning.

He lowered his gaze and chewed on his bottom lip. Then he pushed down his trunks and handed them to me.

"Thank you." I balled them up and threw them toward the beach. They didn't make it the whole way, but it wasn't like they could disappear. "There. Now you can play, and Daddy will have something nice to look at."

He flushed and swam around me. "Maybe I'll latch on to your back. Then you won't see anything."

I chuckled and sank lower in the water, welcoming his arms around my shoulders. "There's plenty you can do back there too."

"Like what?" he asked curiously. The innocence in his tone... He would never understand what it did to me.

"You can play with Daddy," I suggested. "Explore him with your fingers."

"Oh," he breathed out. "Do you like that?"

"Mmm, very much." I eased off the sandy bottom and swam with him on my back, and every now and then, I felt him bumping against me. "It would be a travesty to waste my body on only stereotypically dominant acts when I can finger myself to orgasm without even touching my cock." I was blessed with a sensitive prostate, something I had discovered years before I learned that I preferred to be in charge.

It'd made it a challenge to find partners when I craved power but wanted to bottom at least as often as I wanted to top. In BDSM, I'd met too many switches, and I'd had to explain that the control never left my grasp. Turning off the dominance was not an option. It was part of who I was, and, for the first time, I opened up about it to Peyton. I shared a bit of my history in the world of kink.

I'd never been at the center of a large community or anything, but I'd had a couple friends who had introduced me to it, and I'd attended an event or a party when my hectic schedule had allowed it. It'd been fun to explore physically, though I believed the theory of it all still appealed the most. Likely because I'd tried to have my cake and eat it too.

"You have to be open and give as much as you want to take," I said. "But back then, I had one foot out the door. I said I wanted something serious, but my heart was never fully invested. Combine that with my sexual orientation and my fetishes and it becomes impossible to get very far."

"I understand." He pressed a kiss to my shoulder blade while one of his hands snaked around my middle. "Where did you work before you got involved with Westwater? Sounds like you've always been a busy man."

"Nothing," I answered. "I've always been at Westwater, but I was a location scout for many years. It was my job to predict where a hotel would do well."

"Huh. And then your grandfather thought you should have a more central role?"

"Exactly." I surprised him by diving underwater, and I heard his yelp as I swam along the pristine ocean floor.

The waves on the surface danced in the sunrays across the white sand, and I drew my fingers through it before I went up again. At the deepest, the cove was no more than five feet. I stood on my toes when Peyton swam into my arms and told me I couldn't get away from him.

I wasn't trying.

He didn't get a tan like I did, but the sun turned him out-of-this-world beautiful in other ways. Faint freckles were appearing over his nose, and his hair had become a shade or two lighter.

Fuck, how I wanted to kiss him.

"What about you?" I murmured. "You're a natural submissive with me. Have you been involved in BDSM before?"

He shook his head. "Not at all. I mean, I haven't lived under a rock—I've known about it. But I don't know. Never really occurred to me to look into it further."

I brushed away his hair from his forehead. "A whole world for you to explore, then."

He shrugged. "Maybe." He tugged at my hand and swam backward, toward the shore. "Come on. I bet you brought something good in that cooler."

Of course I did.

There was a large selection of tropical fruit, fresh bread, juice, vodka, goat cheese, saltines, a bottle of wine, and potato chips. In the heat, I craved everything that had a bit of extra salt to it.

Especially Peyton.

CHAPTER 9.

"I never wanna leave Jamaica." Peyton groaned around a mouthful of pineapple and rolled closer to me.

I smiled sleepily and kept my eyes closed. The bed was admittedly an amazing touch. We'd done a decent job at keeping the sand away too. Peyton had protested at first when I'd directed him to the shower after every dip in the ocean, but now he got it.

"Are you pretending to sleep?" He tapped my nose.

I chuckled drowsily and pulled up a knee along the mattress, and I hugged my pillow to me. "No, I'm just relaxing."

He hummed and crawled half on top of me, dropping a sweet kiss to my spine. "There's another cooler by the ice in the supply closet. It's got your name on it."

"It's dinner." I yawned and pushed out my ass a bit when he ghosted a hand over it. "One of the chefs prepared foil packets with fish, potatoes, and vegetables. We'll throw them on the grill later."

"Oh God, that sounds so good." He was slowly testing the waters, touching me more and more, and I loved feeling the tentativeness in each caress. "I like your ass."

"Thanks, baby. It likes you too."

He snickered and rested his head on my hip. "You barely

have any hair here."

Neither did he, though he wasn't hairy by nature. "I wax it."

"Shit, really? Are you kidding?"

"No? It's hardly groundbreaking. It's the one spot I like to keep hairless, and some of us weren't born with your soft fuzz." I'd spent half a siesta ghosting my knuckles across his perfect ass earlier. He had the finest hairs. Otherwise, smooth as a baby's bottom. I wasn't as lucky in that area. "I go a few times a year. Ass and between-the-cheeks."

He swallowed hard, and he lifted his head off of me. "You're serious," he stated quietly. "You wax...*there*? Like, your actual... you know."

"I believe the word you're looking for is asshole. Yes."

"Jesus," he whispered. His fingers traced the length between my cheeks, and I gave a hum of approval. "Doesn't it hurt?"

"You get used to it." My God, he was teasing me with those maddeningly careful touches. "Peyton, grab the coconut oil from Daddy's bag. It's a small bottle in one of the pockets."

He wanted to see me but clearly needed a nudge. Ordering him to give me a massage would hopefully do the trick.

The best part, coconut oil was edible, and we weren't leaving this beach until one of us had received a thorough tongue-fucking.

Peyton returned within seconds and asked what I wanted him to do.

"Massage my ass," I ordered.

"Yes, sir." He scrambled into position and between my legs.

His poorly hidden eagerness was cute.

"I have a clean bill of health, for the record," I told him. "Just so you don't worry when having fun with me—and the day you're ready for more, I have condoms."

"Oh. I wasn't worried. I'm clean too, though. I got tested once to make strangers around me think I had an active sex life."

I laughed into my pillow. Christ, he was too adorable.

"I shouldn't have said that," he muttered.

"No, I'm glad you did," I chuckled. "That's funny. But you're spending the day with someone whose sole companion for the past three years has been Julia."

"I see." He was pleased about that; I could hear it in his tone. I also heard him open the bottle of coconut oil. "Oh, this is slippery."

"Taste it," I encouraged.

There was a beat of silence before he exclaimed, "It tastes like coconut!" And he said it in the most boyish way that sent a sluggish rush of lust through me. "It's not cold, so I'll just drizzle some, Daddy. Are you ready?"

"I'm ready, sweet boy."

The oil dropped onto my buttocks, quite a lot of it, and his hands followed. At long fucking last. I melted into the mattress and groaned under my breath. He'd thankfully left the timid touches behind, and he kneaded my flesh firmly, deeply, and unhurriedly.

"That feels wonderful, pet."

I would've fallen asleep if I weren't anticipating the moment his last shred of decency took a hike. He was careful not to part my cheeks—yet. But I sensed he was getting there. Every now and then, he stroked his hand down the center and applied a hint of pressure on his middle finger.

"Mmm..." I slowly pushed against his grasp, and on the next upstroke, he slipped his thumbs in between. "You're a good boy. It's always okay to explore and play with Daddy."

He exhaled unsteadily and finally grew bolder. By kneading and massaging my cheeks outward, he parted them properly. Then he slid a lone finger from top to bottom, and I couldn't stop the moan from falling from my lips.

"It's so smooth and soft, Daddy." He touched me again,

gently caressing the opening. "Fuck, that's so hot."

I was going to lose my ever-loving mind.

He kept rubbing my flesh with firm strokes, but he no longer shied away from my center. The opposite. He glided his fingers over with each pass, and his breathing picked up.

So did mine, and I couldn't stay completely still. I moved with him, pressing my erection to the mattress and silently encouraging him to do whatever he wanted.

"S-Sir, can you lift up a little, please?" he asked shakily.

"Anything you want, baby." I couldn't mask the need in my tone. Parting my legs farther, I put some weight on my knees and lifted up enough that I could reach my cock. I stroked it slowly and buzzed with the anticipation. I'd dreamed about his fingers for weeks now. I wanted them inside me.

"Are you also hard, Daddy?"

"So fucking hard," I moaned. I wasn't sure if the bolt of pleasure came from his question or the fact that I could feel his breath on my skin, but either way, it changed the course of my fantasy. "It would make me happy if you kissed me down there."

He sucked in a breath and left a soft trail of kisses from the top of one cheek, leading inward to where I wanted him. A violent shiver ripped down my spine at the first feel of him. His soft lips, his gentle kisses, then the tip of his tongue, circling me, licking over and around.

"Oh my God," he breathed, only to come at me again with much less trepidation. He all but buried his face in my ass and forced his tongue inside me. The sensations short-circuited my damn brain. The wet, soft pressure of his tongue combined with the faint stubble on his chin made me hypersensitive to everything he did.

I fisted my cock and stroked myself harder. "Such a perfect little boy," I said, breathing heavily. "If you keep this up, Daddy will turn into an ass-slut for you."

Peyton moaned and replaced his tongue with two fingers. "Can we do this often, please? I don't want it to be over just because I come in two seconds."

I grinned through a breathy laugh and spread the pre-come over the head of my cock. "We can do this as often as possible. I'm gonna spend so much time with my tongue in your sweet little bottom too."

I'd become so attuned to the patterns of his breathing. It was the easiest way to tell how turned on he was, and he evidently liked what I'd said.

He eased away after another moment, and he applied more oil. At the sound of his needy moan, I glanced back at him. Holy fuck, what a sight. While he rubbed the oil into my ass, he was also jerking his beautiful cock, his skin tight and glistening.

I wanted to watch him masturbate many more times.

Closing my eyes, I saved the memory at the forefront of my mind. I replayed it over and over, his wet fingers squeezing the head, his wrist moving, how he twisted his grip on the downward stroke.

He shifted closer once more, and despite his whispered "oops," there was nothing accidental about how he bumped the tip of his cock against my ass. It was official. I'd gone insane. I would never be able to uphold any promises to myself around this young man. Whatever he wanted, he could take.

"Oops," he whispered again. He rubbed his cock over my asshole, and I emitted a drawn-out groan. At the same time, he whimpered. "*Daddy...*" He pushed forward a little more, and I decided not to say anything. "It wants in here..." He fingered me lightly, then used his cock, just the head, and played around the opening. "Daddy, I'm shaking."

I could feel him.

"Are you turning into a little slut too?"

"Yes! But it's your fault!" He grunted with some petulance

and pressed the tip inside. "Oh my God," he moaned. "*Please. Please, please, please*, it feels so good, Daddy. I'll do anything!"

As if I could say no. He made me just as desperate, and I was already spiraling. The slight burn ignited something I'd never felt on this level before.

"Say you're Daddy's little whore."

"I'm Daddy's little whore," he whined. "I can't help it!" He pushed more. And more. Inch by inch, he filled my ass with his hard cock, and my eyes nearly rolled back at the onslaught of euphoria. "I have to fuck you," he pleaded. "I have to take you, Daddy."

"Take me," I exhaled shallowly.

It was already the single most intoxicating experience I'd had, and he made it even better by unleashing the inner boy in him. He fucked me without mercy, going solely by his physical urges and the mind-set he was in.

I met every thrust and drowned in his desperate sounds.

His walls were down; he was utterly uninhibited and free of filters.

"Thank you, Daddy—thank you for giving me this. I have to, I have to. You feel too good." He slammed into me, and I hissed at the burn. "Oh my God, I want to do this every day and every night forever and ever."

"Jesus Christ," I panted.

I was getting close but wanted to prolong the moment, so I released my cock and fisted the sheets. I served up my ass on a platter for him, and he took it. He took it with wild, irregular thrusts, with his fingers digging into my hips, with the head of his cock rubbing against my prostate whenever he hit the wrong angle that felt so goddamn right.

A couple short minutes later, he came with a hoarse cry and collapsed on top of me as his cock pulsed with each release.

I didn't give him half the recovery time he needed. Once his orgasm was over, I manhandled him into the middle of the mattress. I kneeled right there, cradling his head in my hands, guiding him to my cock, and pushed it between his lips when he gasped for air.

"You took what you wanted," I said, out of breath. "It's my turn. Suck my cock, little slut."

He whimpered and wrapped his lips around me, trying to suck me and collect his breath at the same time. Then his hands came around my thigh, and he hugged himself closer to me, clinging to me.

"That's it. That's a perfect little cocksucker." I pushed my cock in and out of his warm, wet mouth. "Fucking hell, you drive me crazy. I've got your come dripping out of my ass. Do you know how that feels?"

He choked around me when I rubbed the head of my cock against the back of his throat.

"Shh, sweet boy. Breathe through your nose. You're doing such a good job." I couldn't believe my luck with this boy. He still wanted more. His fingers crept between my ass cheeks, and he slid two fingers inside me as he coated my cock with his tongue. "Oh God, that's fucking amazing," I moaned. "Do you feel the mess you made in Daddy's ass?"

He hummed and nodded quickly, his big, gorgeous eyes fixed on my face.

"We're going to make a lot of messes together." I stroked his cheek lovingly. "But not this time, because you're gonna swallow every drop I give you, aren't you?"

He nodded again, and the need in his expression meant everything. He sucked and suckled as if he was trying to force the orgasm out of me. And maybe he was.

All thoughts came to a screeching halt, and I gasped. "Right there, Peyton. Right fucking there."

He rubbed persistently at my prostate, and the intense ecstasy crashed down on me.

I screwed my eyes shut and went rigid; every muscle in my body tensed up, and I started coming. I forced myself a little deeper, and there it was. His tight throat squeezed the head of my cock as rope after rope of come shot from me.

I couldn't breathe.

I couldn't move.

Peyton had to feel this soon. He had to know the absolute pleasure of having two orgasms at once. Because that was exactly what it was like. All the tension, all the pressure—it just drained out of my body.

When it was over, all I could do was fall down on the mattress and pull him with me.

I held him to me. I breathed him in.

He buried his face against my neck and mumbled that I had ruined him.

"In a good way, I hope," I murmured drowsily and shuddered.

"The best," he croaked.

We had our last swim in the ocean at sunset while our dinner was on the grill. After that, we showered and got dressed before we settled in to eat. The dining area consisted of seat cushions on the sand and a low table, and we sat next to each other so we both had the spectacular view of the horizon.

Splashes of purple and blue met the fiery sea of red and orange at the bottom.

Peyton took a couple pictures while I poured us some wine.

"What a time to be alive," he murmured. "Can we take one photo together?"

"Of course." I smiled as he flipped his phone to selfie mode and held up his wineglass. Then I leaned into him and pressed a kiss to his temple.

An extra flush of pink graced his sun-kissed cheeks when I eased away.

"Perfect," he whispered, inspecting the picture. "We gotta toast to this. To an amazing day."

"To an amazing day," I echoed and clinked my glass to his. "I can think of no better way to end it than dinner on the beach and you signing another contract."

Amusement filled his green eyes, and he offered a strange look. "What else can I possibly sign away?"

I smirked.

Your life, darling boy.

Ah, if only I could go that far.

"A contract is a bit of a stretch," I amended with a chuckle. "Your signature on a napkin would only be for me." I slipped it out of my pocket and unfolded it next to him. "Just sign here at the bottom when you agree."

"You're certain I will?" He grinned and peered closer to see what I'd scribbled on it. It wiped away his grin in a heartbeat, and I had to laugh at his sweet embarrassment.

It was a single sentence.

I, Peyton Dylan Scott, hereby submit to shower with my owner, Edward Francis Delamare, every morning so he can prepare my ass for his cock.

I extended a pen to him.

He didn't pretend to hesitate, nor did he ask any questions. He grabbed the pen and gave me his signature, all while blushing furiously.

What a time to be alive, indeed.

CHAPTER
10.

We were going to need boundaries.

Having a sex life again—with my assistant, no less —was affecting my work.

In the following week, Peyton and I took advantage of every moment of privacy we were granted. His shyness for everything we'd already tried had vanished, and he had no problem whispering his needs in my ear. Like on our last day in Jamaica when he begged to "kiss Daddy down there again." Or the day after we'd arrived in the Cayman Islands and we had our hotel suite to ourselves for a morning that quickly morphed into afternoon. We ordered room service and sixty-nined each other into oblivion.

A couple days after that, I bent him over the table in the private space in the back of the plane—on our way to Turks and Caicos—and tongue-fucked his ass while he masturbated and came on the carpet.

I had him clean it up on all fours before he sucked me off.

Returning to reality was going to feel like a cold shower, but first, we had one more week in the Bahamas.

Peyton and I arrived at our Westwater resort outside of Freeport in the early afternoon. Mathis was escorting Cathryn and Julia in town, because they'd wanted to stay back and shop for a while.

By now, Peyton had learned that all our resorts looked much the same. Low buildings and bungalows that could withstand hurricanes better, seclusion, golf courses, spas, and so on. The interior design was similar in each location too, with a few exceptions. The bungalows here outside of Freeport were painted in bright colors instead of our standard white, and I had let Julia decide our color. Purple. Because the pink bungalows had been too far away from the pool area.

"Our first meeting was at four, correct?" I double-checked and eyed my watch.

"Yes, sir, and I received the survey from headquarters when we landed," he said. "I'll make copies at the office in the main building before dinner. Then the staff will have two days to hand them in at the lobby."

"Good." I nodded and carried my luggage into the main suite. It was a family-sized bungalow this time, so Julia and I would share my bedroom; Cathryn got her own, Peyton would sleep on the sofa bed in the living room, and Mathis had a room reserved in the main building. "Can you grab Julia's case, please?"

"Yes, sir." He followed me into the bedroom.

"I'm going to ask Cathryn to suggest a movie marathon for Julia tonight," I mentioned. "If she falls asleep in Cathryn's room, I want to spend the night with you."

So far, we hadn't gotten the chance, and I longed for it.

"Okay." Peyton smiled to himself as he stowed away Julia's booster seat.

I blew out a breath and shrugged out of my suit jacket. It was hot; the AC had been thrumming along on the lowest setting until we'd entered. A shower was in order. It would be good to feel refreshed before the meeting in two hours.

"Do you want me to bring your toiletries to the bathroom, sir?"

"Please do. Both of them, and then you can stay in there. We're taking a shower."

He wasted no time, though he hollered from the bathroom that we'd both shaved yesterday—in case I had forgotten. But I had something else in the second toiletry kit that he hadn't seen yet. It wasn't only my shaving essentials.

"I'm aware, little one." I stifled a yawn and removed my tie, then the rest of my clothes. I had a headache that I hoped a quick orgasm would take care of. Unfortunately, it wouldn't be a very pleasurable experience for my boy, but he'd thank me later.

As I entered the bathroom, my mouth twisted up at the sight of Peyton. He'd already shed his clothes, and he gave me an innocent look.

"What?" He stepped closer and grabbed my hand. "I wanna lick you. Come on."

I chuckled softly and cupped his cheek. "Have I told you how adorable you are lately? I don't think there will be time for that, but if you're a good boy, I *might* suck you off."

"Fine—okay." He nodded and remained close to me as I walked over to the counter. His hands never left me, and I fucking loved it. He wrapped his fingers around my soft cock while I unzipped the toiletry case. "I like touching you, Daddy."

"I know, baby. I love that you do." I threaded my fingers through his hair and guided his head to my chest. He knew what to do. He closed his mouth around a nipple and suckled at me, and I hummed in approval.

In the meantime, I dug out my dildo from the bottom of my kit, as well as the suction cup. Both pieces were colorless and transparent, with the dildo made of soft silicone for a more realistic feel. It was my absolute favorite toy, aside from Peyton.

Eyeing the shower, I was pleased to see a built-in bench in

there. I had one like it at home, though there was nothing wrong with attaching the toy to the wall. This was, however, easier.

"Mmm, that feels nice." I kissed the top of his head as he sucked on my other nipple. He had his eyes closed and looked so content to just suck me and play with my cock. It was one of the reasons I wanted to share a bed with him at night. Peyton was obsessed with using his mouth, and I had a cock I wouldn't mind letting him use as a pacifier. "You have a serious case of oral fixation, did you know that?"

He hummed and swiped his tongue around my nipple.

I shivered at the sparks his dirty ministrations shot through me, and I had to stop him before he made me change my plans yet again. "That's enough from that sweet little mouth." I cupped his face and kissed his cheek, lingering a couple seconds, then tilted his head toward the counter. "Look what we're gonna play with. You take my fingers and tongue so perfectly now that it's time to use toys." Three fingers, to be exact. For the past two days, I'd fucked him with three fingers in the shower until he'd pumped his orgasms down my throat.

"Fuck, that's gonna hurt," he responded warily. The delightful blush was back on his face, as were the goose bumps across his shoulders.

His body betrayed his fear, and I brushed my fingers along his hard cock. "I think you'll learn to love it as much as I do."

He swallowed audibly and flicked me an uncertain glance. "You use this a lot?"

"At home—before I had you." I nodded. "It made my evening showers a lot more exciting."

It was sort of sad that it had been one of my personal highlights of the day. Once Julia was asleep, I had my date in the shower.

"That's hot," he whispered under his breath, eyeing the dildo.

"I'll show you when we get home. You can watch me play with myself." I smoothed back his hair.

He nodded. "I want that, but I'm not sure I'd be able to stay away."

I smirked softly and rubbed his neck affectionately. "You'll do whatever the fuck I tell you to, my darling boy. I own you, remember?"

"Oh my God." He plastered himself to me and buried his face against my neck. "I want you so much, Daddy."

I hummed and hugged him to me, then dropped my hand to his delectable buttocks. As I spread his cheeks and teased his hole, I murmured, "And Daddy wants this virgin little ass full of come. Let's get started."

"One more inch, Peyton." I stepped under the hot spray of water and washed away the shampoo in my hair.

My boy was being whiny.

Not only had he used up half a bottle of lube, but he was complaining about pain he was barely feeling. I'd be more inclined to believe him if he weren't eye-fucking my cock like it was a tall glass of water in the desert. A cock that was thicker than that dildo he was failing to sit on.

"How are you going to handle my cock if you can't handle the toy?" I asked.

"You'll make it work," he said flippantly.

"Oh, I definitely will. But it would be nice to minimize your pain," I pointed out.

He gritted his teeth and screwed his eyes shut. With his hands planted firmly on his knees, he tried to lower himself onto the silicone cock that was attached to the marble bench.

"You have to relax, little one." I turned the shower to the

rain setting, then walked over to him. "Bear down on the toy as if it's Daddy's cock." Gripping the base of my semi-erection, I guided it to his lips. "Open up."

He latched on like a needy baby and batted away my hand so he could hold it himself.

I sighed contentedly and eased myself deeper into his mouth.

Sex had never been this amazing before. Peyton's deep-rooted desire to please, not to mention how fully he threw himself into every sexual act, made me feel worshiped and coveted. He was always reaching for me, just like I reached for him. We had this explosive chemistry, and we clicked so well.

"Fuck the toy, Peyton," I murmured huskily. "You can go slowly if you want, but I want to see that beautiful body move up and down." I caressed his face and neck, and I gently wiped away the waterdrops clinging to his eyelashes. "Pretend it's Daddy's cock you're riding."

It seemed to work after a while. He was beginning to relax, and maybe it helped that he concentrated more on sucking me off. It distracted him from the pain, I was guessing.

"That's better," I praised. "You're almost taking all of it now. Maybe you'll be begging for my cock before we get to Nassau on Thursday."

He nodded and redoubled his efforts, fucking himself on the dildo and hollowing out his cheeks around my cock.

I succumbed to the sensations and let them wash over me. Closing my eyes, I pushed myself in and out of his needy mouth until I came in hot spurts.

Peyton could wait. I loved it when he was desperate for me, and he'd be struggling not to be clingy while we worked if I didn't let him come.

"Sir, there's an email from Mr. Brooks with the Three Dots Agency," Peyton said. "It looks like it contains a pitch. Do you want me to print it for you?"

"No, that's fine. I can read it here." I extended my hand, and he gave me my work phone. We'd reached our last day outside of Freeport and had just a quick meeting with the hotel manager left. We were on our way to the hotel restaurant to meet with him right now, but I'd been looking forward to Bennett's ideas. As we turned onto the path weaving between the bungalows and the main building, I scanned the email and felt my interest pique with each sentence.

The man had done his research, and he was continuing to do so. He was letting me know this was just the first proposal.

I wasn't sure it would be needed, frankly. His vision of what Westwater could be... I truly liked it.

"'Beyond the brochure,'" I read, nodding to myself. Bennett wanted to show how Westwater could protect local culture instead of blending in or, worse, fitting the image of those corporations that tried to erase it.

Going local could, in his words, involve everything from cooperating with local businesses, highlighting what a city had to offer—be it through art on the walls, history, or the food we served and the toiletries we provided in the rooms—to emphasizing that we didn't merely protect the local heritage; we *were* the locals. Our staff was always local. There was a stock photo of a woman throwing a smile over her shoulder, the focus being on the print on the back of her polo.

"Ask me about my favorite sushi place in town."
Bennett listed a selection of alternatives.
"Ask me about the best times to visit museums."
"Ask me what time you can catch the sunrise."
"Ask me about the next food festival."

I rubbed my mouth and glanced up; we were almost at the restaurant, and then I returned my attention to the email.

I saw the issues, of course. These changes were expensive, and there was always a backlash when major companies tried to fit in while wearing a tiara, so to speak. But Bennett was on to something worth fleshing out. Technically, the concept wasn't new—even for us. In some of our more exclusive locations, we already collaborated with other brands—although they tended to be of the high-end variety, such as shower products and artisanal refreshments.

The email went on for several paragraphs, but I had to pause here for now. Right where Bennett explained that the personalized uniforms could be replaced or combined with framed signs at the check-in counter, in the elevators, et cetera, depending on the location and the brand of hotel.

Something to consider, definitely.

Peyton opened the door to the restaurant, and I nodded in thanks and welcomed the blast of the colder air that the ceiling fans sent my way.

Guests were enjoying a late lunch in the dining area that opened up to a large patio. The hostess desk caught my attention, and I thought, yes, there could be a small sign encouraging the guest to ask the hostess about her favorite meal, or perhaps her favorite dessert.

"I see Mr. Poitier over there, sir." Peyton gestured toward the patio.

"Lead the way, then, love."

He sent me a curious little smile but made no mention of my slip.

I was suddenly in a good mood. Bennett's email was inspiring me, and more than that, it was reminding me of the fact that I actually loved my job. The biggest bonus walked slightly ahead of me, and perhaps I shouldn't be calling him love during work hours, but fuck it.

"What's it say theu?" Julia pointed at the document I was reading.

"It says that Daddy deserves ice cream after dinner," I replied.

We would be landing in Nassau shortly, and I'd gotten absolutely nothing done during our flight, because my daughter was slipping into a familiar phase where she started screaming if she couldn't sit on my lap. And by "sit on my lap," I meant "climbing all over me," naturally.

It'd been a long month, and it was wearing on Julia. No amount of pool fun or shopping for souvenirs and candy we didn't have in Boston could eliminate the fact that she missed the stability of being at home.

In fact, the traveling was beginning to wear on all of us. Well, except for Mathis. He would spend his life on the road if he could.

"Me too!" Julia said. "Does it say I can have ice cream too? Right theu?" She pointed at a graph on the document.

"Yes." I nodded. "That's exactly what it says, darling."

She nodded too. "Good."

I smiled and gave her a smooch. "Are you ready to return to your seat? We're landing soon."

"The pilot hasn't said nothing." She'd picked up on that, huh? Terrific. Julia kneeled on my lap and looked out the window. "Only water out here, Daddy. Peyton tolded me the blue is water. It's the ocean. It's so big!"

I glanced over at Peyton, who was watching her with a fond little grin.

If I was in trouble before, it had nothing on now. In the past three or four days, I'd started listening to archived episodes of his radio show by the pool and before bed. He was such a passionate historian, and he was funny too. Engaging. Animated. His storytelling had me hooked.

He liked working for me; he'd enjoyed his job at Hilton, too, but I couldn't see his future as easily as I did when I listened to his show. I could picture him in a classroom full of high school students with perfect clarity, however. He'd thrive there one day, when he was ready.

In the meantime, I supposed all I could do was hope for the best while I fell recklessly in love with my assistant.

I didn't have any work commitments the first day in Nassau, so I suggested we all have dinner together in the restaurant by the biggest pool. We'd been spoiled by fantastic seafood all month, but this resort actually had a great pizza-and-burger place to cater to the many families that stayed here. It was, in general, a more family-friendly paradise. Several pool areas, activity clubs for children as well as teenagers, and free transfer into town that was fifteen minutes away.

Julia jumped from lap to lap throughout the evening. Right now, she was helping Peyton finish his pepperoni pizza and interviewing him about his beer and why there were water droplets on the outside of the glass.

Cathryn swayed lightly to the music playing and watched the couples on the dance floor with a soft smile.

I made a mental note to dance with her later. She'd married the love of her life, but he happened to hate dancing.

"Damn," Mathis said, reading something on his phone. He

grimaced. "You're gonna like this, boss. My youngest nephew's decided he's gonna start playing football this fall."

I grinned and tossed a crust onto my plate. "He'll be a Patriot in no time, then. Good."

"Gross," Peyton muttered with a wince.

I shot him a look while Mathis laughed.

"Don't tell me you're a Seahawks fan," I told the punk.

Peyton raised his brows. "What else would I be? Of course I am."

Mathis tipped his beer as a silent hear-hear. He was one of those "Anyone but the Patriots" guys. Originally from Philly, he grew up hating Boston teams. Then his brother moved to Boston when he got married, and since their parents weren't around any longer, Mathis had joined them once he left the Army. He claimed it'd been a full-time job to make sure his two older nephews didn't get sucked in by the Boston spirit, and he'd succeeded quite well. But the youngest already liked the Red Sox.

"Do you guys hang out outside of work?" Peyton asked us curiously.

Cathryn snorted. "Edward doesn't have a social life."

"That's an exaggeration," I argued. Julia slid off Peyton's lap and climbed up on mine instead. "I meet up with you for happy hour sometimes." And she and Tom dragged me over for barbecues in the summer. That was something.

"I'm not sure twice a year qualifies as sometimes," Cathryn drawled.

Of course it did. "I'm not leaving this one with my parents, that's for sure." I smoothed back Julia's messy waves and kissed her forehead. She was getting tired. "She'd come home popping Xanax and drinking martinis."

It was my mother's favorite hobby. I loved her, and my father, but they were the very epitome of the country club people I tried to avoid. If my mother had a martini in one hand and Julia was running toward her, Mother's free hand was used to point at the maid.

Not that Julia would run toward her.

"You could invite Mags to town more often," Cathryn pointed out gently. "Like I said, her watching Julia twice a year is hardly *sometimes*."

I suppressed my flinch and took a swig of my beer instead. We were getting too personal. "She sees her for Easter too," I muttered.

Peyton looked understandably confused, and Cathryn was seemingly in a sharing mood.

"She's Sandra's mother," she explained, which didn't help Peyton at all. So, Cathryn sent me a perplexed look before turning to Peyton again. "Sandra was the little one's mom."

"Oh." Peyton furrowed his brow.

I sighed and glanced over my shoulder toward the bar. We needed new drinks over here.

"So, anyway." Mathis was going to change the topic and ease the tension the only way he could. Bull-in-a-china-shop style. "The boss and I have a standing tradition. We get together at his place for the Super Bowl, the Stanley Cup final, and the World Series."

No one responded to that.

Julia was falling asleep on my chest, so I couldn't count on her for a distraction or diversion.

I was contemplating waking her up to ask if she wanted that ice cream, but then a server arrived, and there was a collective rush of relief from all of us. Except Peyton. Something had soured his mood.

Goddammit.

It was up to me, which I suspected was Cathryn's choice.

She was otherwise wonderful at steering conversation into safer waters.

Peering down at Julia, I figured there was one thing I could do. Perhaps Peyton was holding back the parts of his history because I was doing the same. Maybe he thought I had trust issues; I didn't. Maybe he did, though. For me, it was merely a time of my life that brought pain and grief.

"Mind if we move this party to the terrace?" I asked. "I'm going to put this little monkey to bed."

"Sounds like a good idea." Cathryn nodded. "Anything we can do?"

"Yes, bring alcohol." I was going to need it when I reemerged. "You can come give me a hand, Peyton."

"Yes, sir," he responded politely. Too politely.

I'd never told him that he could call me by my name after work hours.

CHAPTER
II.

"I'm not tired," Julia whined.

"Of course you're not, darling." I helped her change clothes, and her head popped up from her pajama shirt. "It's been a while since I told you the story of us."

She nodded sleepily and pulled on the bottoms.

Peyton stood in the doorway, but I did my best not to focus on him.

"Tell it, Daddy." She jumped over to her pillow and plopped down and under the duvet. "It starts wiv Daddy and Mommy S in school."

I smiled and crawled over to lie down in the middle. It was easier if I could turn my back on the doorway. "Yes. They were the best of friends and grew up together." I pulled up the duvet to her chin and tucked her in properly. "They thought it was funny that they were so alike while being so different at the same time. They had the same hobbies, spent all their time together, liked the same subjects in school, and were accepted at the same college."

"But Daddy liked boys, and Mommy liked girls," she recited.

I chuckled quietly and combed back her hair a bit. "That's

right, and in college, Mommy S met her first girlfriend, Mommy M."

"Tha's when Daddy got mad." Julia made a scowl, presumably to mimic me.

"He did. It wasn't his proudest moment," I admitted. "He was just afraid that Mommy S would forget Daddy, but he shouldn't have worried. He became great friends with Mommy M too."

The heaviness landed on my heart like I knew it would. I still saw us, the three of us, back then. Fresh out of college, traveling together, them trying and failing to hook me up with someone, me trying and *succeeding* to play peacemaker when they'd argued. Sandra, with her calm demeanor, dirty-blond waves, blue eyes, and the biggest stubborn streak in history. Then Mona. A fiery brunette with Italian roots, a loud mouth, short fuse, and yet, so much patience. She could never hold a grudge.

"They were the best friends Daddy could ever ask for," I went on, swallowing the emotions that rose. "And one day, when they asked Daddy to help them have a baby, he didn't even think about it. He said yes right away."

Julia turned onto her side and closed her eyes, searching me out with her hand. She played with my earlobe. "Then Daddy was silly again."

"Was he?"

She nodded. "Cuz he say he wanted only to be an uncle."

I grinned. "That's true. It was very silly of him." Christ, I'd been naïve. Mona hadn't thought much of it, but Sandra had known me better than I'd known myself. The two had wanted to raise a baby together, without a father involved, and I'd been wholly on board. Family hadn't existed on my radar. "The three of us agreed that Daddy would stay close, but Mommies would raise the baby together. And we were all excited. We went to the doctor together, and Daddy only missed one single appointment."

Julia hummed. It was usually her favorite part, though she was too tired now.

"One day, Daddy came over to Mommies' apartment." I stroked her cheek gently, the memories still so fucking vivid. "He wanted to know how the doctor's appointment had gone, and he almost stumbled right there at the door."

"Shoes," Julia whispered knowingly.

"Mm, he looked down and saw a pair of cute shoes for a girl." I released a breath and rubbed at the tightness in my chest. "He picked them up and stormed into the kitchen, where he found Mommy S and Mommy M. 'We're having a girl?' he asked. And they nodded and beamed brighter than the sun and burst into happy tears. 'We're having a girl!' they said."

Thinking back on it now, I could see where things began to change for me. Finding out the gender had made everything more real. Suddenly, I was picturing glimpses of the future. I was going to teach this little sprite how to cheer for the Patriots, how to ride a bike, and I was going to be there when she took her first steps.

Sandra had seen it and suggested a contract. First and foremost, to make sure I got custody should anything happen to them, and secondly, in an attempt to give me some rights. I'd always liked contracts. They were insurance. They were security. She'd known that too. And so, we signed an agreement that would grant me one weekend a month and a couple weeks in the summer when Julia had grown out of the newborn phase.

Everyone was happy again, and the vise around my chest had loosened.

"The day you were born, it was love at first sight." I gathered Julia's hand and kissed the top of it before I tucked it under the duvet. She was asleep. "I understood that being an uncle and godfather would never be enough."

I'd kept it to myself for three months. Three excruciating months. Then I started planning how to tell Sandra and Mona. Hell, I'd been ready to beg. I'd invited them over for dinner the following weekend.

We never got that far.

Definitely needed a drink now. After kissing Julia on the forehead, I rolled off the bed with a grunt and reluctantly faced Peyton.

I met him in the doorway, where he slipped his hand into mine and looked down at our fingers.

"How did they die?" he asked quietly.

"Car accident. They were out test-driving an ugly fucking minivan."

Julia had been with Sandra's mother for the afternoon.

"I'm so sorry, sir," he whispered.

"Edward." I cleared my throat and peered down at our hands too. "We're off the clock."

"Okay."

I wanted to hear him say it. I wanted to hear my name fall off his lips.

"I need a drink," I said instead. "But now you know."

It was a good thing I didn't know Peyton back then. I'd barely been human. In my darkest days, the guilt had threatened to consume me, and I'd been half convinced that I'd subconsciously wished for Sandra and Mona to die.

I knew better these days, of course, but the mind could play tricks that hurt more than a gunshot wound.

"For what it's worth," he murmured, "your friends couldn't have left Julia in better hands."

I swallowed hard, unable to respond, and lifted his hand and kissed his knuckles. Then I let go and trailed outside.

Four drinks took the edge off.

Cathryn stopped after her last glass of wine and promised she'd move Julia to her bedroom later.

I appreciated it immensely and poured my fifth, this time a rum and no Coke.

Mathis was quizzing Peyton about his radio show. Specifically, the Vietnam War.

"He's done at least four episodes on that," I said. I couldn't know if there were more, as only the past twenty shows were available on the radio network's website.

Peyton grinned curiously. "How would you know?"

"Because I've listened to them." I took a swig. "I like that you go all the way back. Otherwise, you can't understand the war. I've seen so many documentaries that start with JFK, but you have to go back to Woodrow Wilson and when Ho Chi Minh tried to meet with him—and you do that."

Mathis nodded in agreement. "I'll have to check them out."

I tipped my glass at Peyton, who was watching me with a pinch of amusement and wonder. "You should host your own podcast instead. You'd have a much bigger reach." Fuck, I almost spilled. Almost. I didn't. "He's amazing," I told Mathis. "He had me hooked after five minutes."

"Christ," Peyton chuckled. The sweet boy was blushing. "How many drinks have you had?"

"As long as I can keep track, not enough." I winked.

I was intoxicated but not drunk. Yet. I was just...loosening up a bit. Thinking about Sandra and Mona required some therapy afterward, and this was therapy. Sitting out here on the terrace, hearing music from the pool area, other guests enjoying their vacations around us... I felt better now.

Mathis stole Peyton's attention again with more questions about war history, and I stole the bag of chips on the table.

"I think that's my cue to say goodnight," Cathryn decided. "It's enough that I have to listen to Tom go on and on and *on* about World War II."

"Tom's a good man," I replied with a nod.

"He has his moments." Cathryn smirked wryly and dipped down to kiss my cheek. "Go get him, Edward."

Oh, of course she knew. I shook my head but couldn't help but smile.

"Goodnight, everyone." She picked up her sandals and headed inside.

"Night, dear. I owe you a dance," I told her.

"I don't know what for, but I'll hold you to it." She grinned and slid the door closed.

Mathis, Peyton, and I spent the next hour or so lost in conversations about the historical events and people we admired and were fascinated by one way or another. Peyton and I had a lot in common, particularly where World War II was concerned, but where he went full-on adorable geek on the Civil War and colonial times in Africa, I preferred the political mind games of the Cold War.

Eventually, Mathis declared he was ready to hit the sack, and I looked at my watch. Fucking hell, it was almost two AM.

"When's my first meeting tomorrow?" I asked.

"At ten," Peyton replied. "And they're back-to-back until dinner."

It was going to be a less glamorous day, in other words.

After we said goodnight to Mathis, he headed for his own room, and Peyton and I went inside and took turns in the bathroom. When I came out, I noticed he'd drawn the drapes but hadn't prepared the sofa bed yet. *Good.* I'd already made up my mind, regardless. I grabbed his luggage and wheeled it into my bedroom.

I'd just draped my pants over my own luggage and was unbuttoning my shirt when Peyton poked his head in.

"You stole my bag."

"It was my subtle way of asking if you'd like to spend the night with me."

He smiled and closed the door, turning the lock too. "I was gonna ask you anyway. Well, I was going to make an awkward attempt at seducing you."

I was sort of sad to miss that. I was sure it would've been tremendously Peyton-like and, therefore, impossible to resist.

Pulling my undershirt over my head, I slumped down on the edge of the bed and threw the tank into the closet.

Peyton must've gotten undressed in the bathroom. He was only in briefs and his own undershirt.

He walked over to me and set one knee on the mattress. I took the hint and backed up slightly, then welcomed him onto my lap. Where he belonged. I slipped my hands up his thighs and back to his ass, bringing him closer to me.

He dropped his forehead to mine and closed his eyes.

Fuck, he was beautiful.

Someway, somehow, we had to make it. This wasn't a game for me. Perhaps it had started out as something fun, something casual, but it couldn't stay that way any longer.

I closed my eyes too, and I just breathed him in and let my hands roam his back.

"Edward," he whispered.

I shivered. That felt right. It sounded right. Opening my eyes again, I caught him gazing at my mouth. He ran his knuckles over my stubble and wet his bottom lip.

It was as if my senses went into overdrive. A strong buzz flowed between us, and I reached up and brushed the pad of my thumb over his lip. In turn, he kissed it softly and nuzzled my nose.

I drew a breath as his lips ghosted across mine. The light touch went straight through me, waking up every erogenous zone I had. I slid my hand to the back of his neck and closed the distance again, and our breaths mingled. He parted his lips to capture my upper one between his, and I swiped the tip of my tongue over his bottom one. It was the most tentative first kiss I'd experienced, and yet it was a perfect contrast to how we'd dived in headfirst with everything else.

The second our tongues met, a careful caress, I thought I was going to burst. Lips ghosting, tongues sliding, hands finding purchase. He trembled and locked his arms around my neck, and it did it for me. I angled my head and surrendered. I covered his mouth with my own, and the buzz grew even stronger. I kissed him firmly, passionately, and felt him melt into me.

It wasn't enough.

Needing to consume him, I shifted on the bed so I could lay him down on the mattress, and I followed. I crawled over him, and he scooted farther up, and our mouths never left each other.

"Daddy," he whimpered.

"I'm right here, baby." I kissed him harder, swirling my tongue around his. "Daddy's got you."

He nodded and began squirming himself out his underwear.

I only stopped kissing him to remove his undershirt. Then I was back, and he pushed down my boxer briefs and dug his heels into my ass.

I sucked his bottom lip into my mouth.

He moaned and rubbed his cock against my hip.

"Move," he breathed. He nudged me onto my back and straddled me. There, he pushed my boxer briefs all the way off, and I sat up, capturing his mouth in another deep kiss. He made one of his needy sounds and slid his tongue alongside mine. "It's possible I stashed the bottle of coconut oil under your pillow while you brushed your teeth."

I let out a chuckle and squeezed him to me. "You'd have no issues whatsoever seducing me, Peyton."

"Good." He wriggled his sweet little ass over my cock and kissed me. "I don't wanna wait anymore, Daddy. I want your big cock in me."

I got lost in another dizzying kiss and wrapped my fingers around his cock. "Okay. Let's get you ready. Get on all fours for me."

"*Yesss.*"

His youthful joy turned my cock to granite, and while he scrambled into position, I found the bottle of oil under one of the pillows. Then I crawled behind him and thanked my lucky stars for that magnificent view.

Daddy had to get a taste first.

After spreading a generous amount of oil along his crease, I leaned in and tongue-kissed his little hole. He yelped softly before exhaling a moan and pushing his ass against me.

I hummed and continued eating him out as I coated my cock in oil.

"God, your tongue," he panted.

I loved how I made him squirm.

"Lie down on your back, little one." I gave him one more openmouthed kiss before sitting back on my haunches. He obeyed and turned around, parting his legs like a good boy. "You're perfect." Utterly fucking perfect for me. I lowered myself over his cock and took him in my mouth.

"*Hnngh.*" He fisted my hair and thrust as deeply as he could. "Oh fuck, Daddy." He gasped when I slid my middle finger inside him. "More, please."

I smiled around his cock, sucking at the tip. "My little slut is eager."

"Yes," he groaned. "For you."

Only me.

He took two fingers with ease too, and then three. All while I sucked his cock in long, strong strokes.

His thighs tensing up told me he was getting close already, and it'd be a while before he was allowed to come. So, I released him and poured some more oil over his asshole. He reached for me, a soft "please, please, please" falling from his lips.

Once we were face-to-face, I dipped down and kissed him hungrily.

He clawed at me. He snaked his legs around mine.

He'd waited long enough, and I'd teased him through my preparations for him.

"You're gonna take my cock almost every day from now on." I pinched his bottom lip between my fingers and slid my tongue into his mouth. "One way or another. Are you ready for that?"

"So ready," he exhaled. "I want you to use me all the time."

"We'll use each other," I murmured, guiding the head of my cock to his opening. "Whenever we get needy like this."

He nodded quickly.

I pushed in slowly. "Let Daddy in, baby. Breathe deeply and push back. I'm not going to stop."

"Okay," he whimpered. He licked his lips and threw his head back onto the pillow.

Inch by inch, I claimed him.

Jesus fucking Christ.

I dropped my forehead to his neck once I was buried all the way in, and it took all my restraint to stay still and let him adjust to my size.

Peyton's breaths came out in tiny mewls, a sound that probably shouldn't turn me on so damn much.

"Are you taking the pain for Daddy like a perfect little boy?"

"Yes, Daddy," he whined.

A low growl rumbled from my chest, and I had to move. Never before had I felt this possessive. I withdrew carefully and placed my fingers loosely around his throat, and then I sank into him again.

"Oh God." He gasped and grabbed on to my arms.

"You feel so fucking amazing." I sucked on his neck and fucked him slowly. My thumb brushed over his carotid artery, and I applied the barest hint of pressure. "I love hearing your sounds. Especially when you choke. And when you get so desperate that you whine and whimper."

He hauled in a hoarse breath and sought out my lips.

I kissed him hard and gave him a few shallow thrusts, quicker ones, before I pushed in deep. Swallowing his groan, I reminded him to be quiet.

"We don't want anyone knocking on the door when I'm busy fucking your little bottom."

He shook his head and bit down on his lip. His expression wasn't as pinched now.

"I'm not a virgin that way anymore," he said shyly.

"No, you're not." I touched his cheek affectionately and smiled down at him. "You don't know how stunning you are when you let go of all your filters."

"It's liberating." He screwed his eyes shut in pain when I gave him a particularly sharp thrust. "*Oww.*"

I couldn't help myself. He drove me to the brink of insanity with his boyish behavior.

Peering down between us, I gathered his legs and moved his knees toward his chest. "God, look at you." I stared at my cock disappearing in and out of his wet, warm, tight-as-fuck ass. "Daddy likes it when you squeeze your little hole like that."

"Holy shit," he breathed, eyes wide. "There—right there."

I gripped the backs of his knees and effectively folded him in half, and then I started fucking him faster. I was transfixed. I knew what this angle did to him. I knew what I was rubbing up against, and his cock, which had softened from the pain earlier, was thickening quickly again.

"I'm getting this on video one day soon," I muttered, out of breath. "Fucking hell, I can't look away."

He made it even better when he hooked his arms under his knees. It freed my hands so I could touch him wherever I wanted, and I did. I traced a finger around his opening, I cupped his balls, I stroked his cock, I left fingerprints on his thighs and ass.

"My pretty fuckdoll," I groaned under my breath. "I'm going to play with you every day."

"Can the doll also fuck Daddy?"

"All the fucking time, baby," I promised. "Fuck—I'm gonna come soon." I wasn't ready, goddammit. It was too hot. The pleasure built up too fast. My balls felt full and heavy, and all the fantasies of future playtime made me want to cover him with my come. I wanted pictures of it. Pictures of us. Of me taking him, of him taking me.

Spurred on by his evident excitement and pleading moans, I fucked him into the mattress in quick thrusts. I stopped breathing at some point and felt the orgasm taking over, pushing me down, making me gnash my teeth, causing me to pound into him.

Then I was gone.

I collapsed on top of him and fucked my release deep into his ass in irregular movements.

I didn't know how many seconds I was under, but when my hearing returned, all I heard were his needy pleas.

I blew out a labored breath and eased away carefully. A string of come connected the head of my cock with his bottom, and I shuddered violently. My mouth watered, and, luckily, I could get more of that. It wouldn't take too many seconds either, because as soon as I sucked Peyton's cock into my mouth, he nearly arched off the bed.

"Fill Daddy's mouth, baby boy." I swirled my tongue around him, then took him deep, tasting the salty fluids already trickling from his cock.

His hands disappeared into my hair, and I encouraged him to use me properly. *Let go, pet. Don't hold back.* He was a quivering mess, but he listened. He pulled me down on him and thrust in and out of my mouth, without any finesse whatsoever. And it was probably my favorite thing about when his barriers were down. My little boy chased his orgasm and thought only about the pleasure.

His warm release flooded my mouth a few heartbeats later, and the thick streams slid down my throat with each swallow.

It was the first time he'd reacted so wildly to anything stimulating his prostate, and combined with being taken and then a blow job ending in an orgasm, I saw the emotional release coming before it happened. His shaking wouldn't stop even after he'd finished coming.

After cleaning him up with my tongue, I crawled over him and landed next to him on the mattress. He was quick to fly into my embrace, and I held him to me.

"What the fuck am I doing?" he sniffled, catching his breath. "It felt so good. I don't know why I'm... Fuck."

"You're just overwhelmed, love. It's perfectly normal." I managed to get us under the duvet before I squeezed him to me again. "There we go. I'm not letting you go, I promise."

He nodded and snaked his arm around my middle. "Ever," he croaked.

"Ever," I murmured.

He had to see that we belonged together.

CHAPTER
12.

"Daddy, look!"

"Oh my. That's not a small sundae."

"No, it's a big," she replied frankly.

I grinned and dipped down to kiss the top of her head. She was all cuddled up in her towel, sharing a double lounger with Cathryn. Unlike Peyton and I, who had worked all day, the girls had alternated between going to the beach and being at the pool. Now they were resting up under an umbrella.

"You wanna go in with us, darling?" I asked, draping my towel over the lounger next to theirs. It was also a double, so I nodded for Peyton to place his towel there too.

"Can't. I'm busy." Julia scooped up some ice cream. "Cathryn finds funny videos on de iPad."

Cathryn handed over the tablet, presumably having found something new on YouTube for her. "Here you go, honey. There are a few videos cued up."

I smiled at my girl. It would do her well to head home soon, but no one could say she hadn't been enjoying herself this month.

Peyton rounded our lounger and squatted down to whisper something in Julia's ear.

She cocked her head. "Really?"

He nodded.

She grinned goofily. "Me too."

What had he said to her?

Peyton looked like he'd won the lottery as he rose and aimed for the pool. He tightened the drawstrings on his trunks, then dove into the deep end.

I followed.

After six meetings with everyone from the manager, front office manager, staff, and a local advertising firm, I was beyond ready to wash this day away. Wearing a suit in eighty-five-degree heat truly did suck.

The water cleared my head in an instant, and I resurfaced a few feet away from Peyton.

Most of the guests around us were getting ready for dinner, so we shared the pool with only one other couple.

Now there was a good word. Peyton and I weren't a couple yet, with emphasis on yet.

Considering how we'd woken up together this morning, there was no other alternative. We'd gotten five minutes of cuddling and a wonderful, lazy make-out session before work called, and it'd sealed the deal for me. I was making my intentions clear tonight after dinner.

"What were you and Julia whispering about?" I asked.

He smirked and shrugged. "Secret."

I narrowed my eyes.

He lowered his mouth to the surface of the water and swam closer. "Here's a subtle topic change. I can't stop thinking about last night. Kissing you...having you inside me..."

Subtle, perhaps not, but effective.

"I should've kissed you weeks ago." Fuck, I wanted to touch him, but if I knew Cathryn, she was keeping an eye on us.

Some confidence left Peyton's eyes. "Why didn't you? You

don't strike me as a man who'd chicken out—like I've done. I was too much of a coward to initiate it. I kept thinking, maybe it's too intimate for him, maybe he reserves that for real relationships..."

I didn't want him to think any of those things. It bothered me more than I thought it would. So, I supposed we were having this conversation right here and right now. Fine by me.

"First of all, what you and I have is real," I told him quietly but seriously. "Secondly, it wasn't intentional at first—not consciously anyway. I do like catching you off guard, and a kiss is usually what you begin with."

Heat bled across his cheeks. I hoped he was remembering the night he came into my bedroom at home and watched me masturbate, because that was a memory I wouldn't change for anything.

"It felt natural and exciting to explore your body first." I was hopeless. Even here, this second, it was turning me on to the point where I had to adjust my cock. "Then I thought more and more about it when we got to the islands. It became the piece that was missing."

He nodded slowly and circled me.

I twisted my body to face him, and I pushed my hair back. "But perhaps I'm not as brave as you might believe, because when we visited the private beach and you expressed gratitude for the adventure I was giving you, chickening out was essentially what I did. It gave me a reality check—that this was possibly just fun for you. So, I decided to wait a while as I got my wits about me."

"Oh." He furrowed his brow. "Did you get your wits about you?"

I shook my head.

"And what does not getting your wits about you entail, exactly?"

I grinned softly at his endearing apprehension. He wouldn't

145

make direct eye contact at the moment, finding the bottom of the pool a seemingly interesting spot to stare at.

"It entails quite a bit," I admitted. "For instance, thinking about you constantly. Wanting to know everything about you. Waking up with you next to me." Nervousness tightened my gut as quickly as it disappeared when he met my gaze with hope and relief in his eyes. "Taking you out to dinner." His hand found mine under the surface, and I pulled him a little closer. "Kissing you in public."

He exhaled shakily and slid a hand up on my back. With the sun beating down on my shoulders and neck, his touch was cold and shiver-inducing.

"Making you mine in every sense of the word," I finished. My heart started beating faster at the reminder of how publicly I was declaring this. He needed to know the seriousness of everything before I kissed him. "Is this something you're interested in?"

He let out a breathy laugh and shook his head. "You have no idea."

My heart kept hammering as the euphoria coursed through me. "I won't involve my daughter in anything that isn't serious."

He nodded once, a quick one in understanding. "I don't know how to explain what I feel without freaking you out, but you haven't left my mind since the day you walked into the International and asked about recruiting me." He swallowed and wet his bottom lip. "I guess there's only one contender." And when he flicked a glance toward Julia, it made my whole day. "You've both turned my world upside down."

I closed my eyes in contentment and pressed my forehead to his.

"Can we go out soon?" he asked hesitantly. "I have some things I'd like to get off my chest, and I don't want to get my hopes up in case you hear something that changes anything for you."

I opened my eyes again and frowned in confusion.

"I haven't been open about..." He trailed off and rubbed the back of his neck. "I don't know. It's just bugging me."

"What could possibly change how I feel about us?" I asked.

"My background?" He phrased it as a question for some reason. "It doesn't look good to begin with, and less so if I start dating my multimillionaire boss."

Oh, for heaven's sake.

I cupped his cheeks and made him face me. "Peyton, I hired you without even looking at your resumé. Do you honestly believe I give a shit about image?"

"Maybe not, but—"

"No buts." I closed the distance and kissed him firmly. "We'll have dinner tomorrow, just you and me. A proper date. But don't think for a second that you need to have a fucking pedigree to date me. I've run away from that lifestyle once already."

"Pedigree," he chuckled uncomfortably.

I smiled in sympathy, seeing how much this bothered him. "I'm serious, baby. Whatever it is, I...I don't think I will be shocked. I have my own theories already."

He bit his lip. "About my mom?"

I nodded with a dip of my chin. "I've been leaning toward rehab or prison time."

He flushed instantly and averted his gaze, and the glassiness in his eyes got caught in the reflection of the sun.

"Am I close?" I murmured.

He swallowed and nodded. "Both."

Ah.

"Leave everything about tomorrow to me. We'll go someplace private." I hugged him to me and pressed my lips to his temple. "You can tell me whatever you want. It won't change the fact that you're mine. Okay?"

He wrapped his arms around my middle and nodded against my neck. "Yes, sir, but I'll understand if—"

"Daddy!" Julia hollered.

"Well. She picked a good time to interrupt," I said with another kiss to Peyton's temple. "You were undoubtedly about to say something idiotic."

Peyton spluttered a chuckle.

"*Daddy!*" Julia's voice rose to shrill and demanding, and I turned toward her just in time to see her running off her lounger. It happened so fast, but thankfully, my instincts kicked in. Processing came later. She tumbled toward the edge and darted straight out into the water.

Peyton and I both kicked off from the bottom of the pool and dove under a fraction of a second after Cathryn bolted from the lounger with a shout.

Julia hadn't reached the bottom yet when I grabbed on to her arm and hauled her up, and *that* was when my pulse skyrocketed.

She coughed and choked.

"Daddy's got you." I blew out a heavy breath and patted her firmly on the back. Water was coming out of her nose, and she'd probably inhaled a mouthful. I nodded to Cathryn that I had it covered; she could fuss later. "That's good, darling. Just cough until it feels better."

Cathryn stayed in the background with a hand on her chest.

I sat Julia down on the edge of the pool and rubbed her back. The worst seemed to be over. Good, because she was about to get an earful from me. Christ, this girl. She was too reckless.

"Better?" I brushed some water away from her face.

She coughed and nodded.

Peyton took that as a sign to move forward. He cupped her cheeks and kissed her on the forehead. "You sweet little terror, what have we said about going into the pool without asking first?"

"I have impowtant question 'bout ice cwream," she argued in a croak.

"That doesn't matter," he told her. "You ask first. Unless Daddy, Cathryn, or I tell you it's okay to jump in, you stay put."

Or maybe I would just shut up, because Peyton was evidently handling it.

"But Daddy catches me!" she exclaimed. "He always does."

"It's still a rule we've given you," Peyton reminded her seriously. "We follow rules, don't we?"

I rubbed a hand over my mouth to hide my smile, and I glanced up and exchanged a look with Cathryn. She saw it too, and she grinned slightly.

"But he was right there," Julia whined.

"And what if we hadn't heard you?" Peyton countered. He was patient with her but didn't let her off the hook. "A hundred things can go wrong, sweetheart. That's why you *have* to wait. You have to. All right?"

"Fiiine!" She huffed and turned to me. "Tell him to stop yelling at me."

I raised a brow at her, ticked off. "That's not yelling. *I* would've yelled at you. You want me to do that?"

She sucked her bottom lip into her mouth and shook her head. I hoped she realized there would be no turning the adults against one another.

"You're going to bed early tonight, and no dessert after dinner," I said.

The world came to an end for Julia there, and Daddy was suddenly the meanest person ever.

Daddy could live with that.

The next day, I got a rare chance to take an actual nap. It started out with Julia next to me, but she woke up before I did, and Cathryn left a note saying they'd gone to the mini golf course on the property.

My workday was over, and Peyton was nowhere to be seen, so I took a shower and got dressed. Cargo shorts and a button-down would do for a casual date. Considering Peyton wanted to get something "off his chest," I hadn't made any grand plans. Instead, I'd packed a daypack with a blanket, a bottle of rum, and some snacks. On the way out, we'd pick up dinner from the restaurant, which reminded me—I had to call and place my order.

"Boss, you in there?" Mathis called from the terrace.

I crossed the living room and poked my head out. "Well, there's one of you. Have you seen Peyton?"

He jerked his chin in the general direction of...elsewhere. *Everything* was where he nodded. "I saw him in the office earlier."

Ah, so the main building.

Mathis sat down in one of the chairs and lit up a cigarette. "Your dry cleaning arrived earlier. That's all I had to say."

"Thank you." I stepped outside and took a seat too. "Do you have any plans for the Fourth of July?"

We'd have one week back home in Boston before we headed out again. But it would be our last extended trip for a while. After a tour of some of our major hotels on the mainland, we'd be home for a couple months.

"I'll be at my brother's, I reckon," he replied. "What about you?"

"Same as always, I suppose. Trent's family picnic." My cousin and his wife went all out for the holiday. I mostly went because Julia loved to spend time with Trent's girls. They were her age.

Mathis nodded slowly and took a drag from his smoke.

"You invitin' Peyton?" he asked with a smirk.

I chuckled. "I wish, but he'll be with his own family." It'd come to no one's surprise yesterday when Peyton and I had shown some PDA at the pool and later at dinner. "He'll fly straight to Seattle when we get to Miami."

I wasn't looking forward to that, even though I understood him. I was just being selfish. I'd promised him we'd make sure he could see his family once a month, "give or take," and it'd been almost two since he'd spent time with them. Additionally, most of his prerecorded episodes on the radio network had aired now, so he'd spend a day in the studio while he was on the West Coast too.

"Speak of the devil." Mathis nodded at something behind me.

I peered over my shoulder and saw Peyton walking toward us. He looked tired, but he smiled when he spotted me.

"You're up." He jogged the last few steps and squeezed my shoulder, then dipped down and kissed me chastely. "How was your nap?"

"Fantastic. They should be a thing for adults, too."

"I hear it works in Spain." He grinned and sat down in the empty chair next to me. "When are we heading out?"

"Whenever you're ready." I grabbed his hand, just because I could, and threaded our fingers together. "I thought I'd pick up dinner before. That's all."

"Perfect. I only need a quick shower. Can we get something greasy from the pool grill?"

I chuckled. "Anything you want."

"Well, aren't you two sickeningly sweet," Mathis drawled.

"Finally! I'm one of those people now," Peyton exclaimed. "Just wait till we get to the office. All his memos will be delivered on pink Post-its with hearts on them."

I laughed and kissed his knuckles.

An hour or so later, we arrived on a secluded part of the beach with one daypack and one to-go bag from the grill.

"I apologize for not being more creative with what I would like to consider our second date."

Our day on the private beach had been too good to waste in the official count.

"This is perfect," Peyton said with a shake of his head. "I just wanna chill with you."

After we got comfortable on the blanket, he tore into our food and devoured a hot dog—off the kids' menu—before I'd even started on a pizza slice.

"What a fucking day," he groaned around his food.

My amusement made way for a pinch of worry. "Did I miss something while I had my beauty sleep?"

He shrugged and grabbed another hot dog, getting mustard and relish on his fingers. "I had a fight with my mom over the phone. All I did was express worry about being away from them for so long, and she laid into me. Said I should stop treating her like a child, which, of course, made me feel guilty and...blah. It's a whole thing between us."

I squeezed his knee and took a bite of my pizza. "Start from the beginning, and then maybe I can help."

If this was rough for him, he didn't show it. Hopefully, my reassurance at the pool yesterday had alleviated his fears. He did look very tired, though.

"I'm gonna go with the shortest version," he said. "Partly because there isn't all that much to say, and partly because I'm better at answering questions than rambling. Unless it's about history."

I smiled softly and nodded for him to go on.

"So, she was a single mom with me for the longest time," he started. "We made it work pretty well, I thought. But she was lonely and exhausted, working three jobs and so on. There's no one else—our family's tiny, even more so after Nana died." He wiped his mouth on a napkin. "Mom met a dude when I was... sixteen, I think. And by dude, I mean a fucking asshole. He and I didn't get along whatsoever. He was a dick to Mom, and she refused to see it."

Having only heard the beginning, it was already easy to see why Peyton had been tired for years. A mental exhaustion that couldn't be treated with a nap. He'd been forced to grow up too early.

"She's always liked to drink with dinner," he went on. "I didn't see it as a problem. It was how I grew up. But then she got pregnant with Anna, and she kept drinking. I confronted her about it, of course, and that's when I noticed that she'd covered a bruise on her arm. I was fucking livid. I had no fuse back then—not when it came to her asshole boyfriend."

He'd stopped eating. Instead, he stared at his hands in his lap. If he'd been a woman, I would've thought he was inspecting his nail polish with how he held them out. But he was studying his knuckles. He drew a finger over a scar I hadn't noticed before.

"You went after him," I concluded quietly.

He nodded. "He worked at a construction site across town,

and I didn't even think. I just drove over there and beat the shit out of him."

Christ.

"He was actually fired," he said. "The official reason was that he drank on the job, which didn't surprise me one bit. What did surprise me was that he cooled down for a while after that. I'd expected him to come after me, but he didn't. He ignored me completely, and I tried not to be around when he was home."

He cracked his knuckles absently and glanced at the horizon where the sun was dipping lower and lower.

"But an abuser never stops when he gets caught," he murmured. "They just change tactics. I wasn't around enough to see it either. I was always at a friend's house or at the Quad."

I cocked my head. "The Quad?"

"Ah, yeah, a place for teenagers. Usually those who don't wanna be at home for one reason or another." He reached for his fountain soda but didn't drink from it. "About a week after Anna was born, I heard them fighting in the living room. He wanted her to shut the baby up."

"Jesus Christ," I whispered, instantly flooded with anger.

"Yeah, sweet guy." He nodded once. "I guess he couldn't maintain the charade any longer—combined with my eyes opening a bit more. He'd never stopped beating her. He'd just gotten better at hitting her where the bruises didn't show." He squinted at something and scratched his forehead. "I'm rambling, aren't I? Can I blame you for drawing it out of me?"

I ignored his weak attempt at humor and gave his knee another squeeze. "You can blame whoever you want, as long as you keep going."

He blew out a breath and nodded slowly. "In short, it was a shitshow after that. I alternated between keeping my mouth shut—so I could be there for Anna—and getting into vicious fights with both him and my mom, because this couldn't go on.

I just watched her sink deeper and deeper into alcoholism, and I asked her what would happen once she got fired. When she could no longer keep a job. And she said she was working on it. She apologized to me over and over, drunk off her ass, looking like a complete fucking mess." He shook his head to himself and scrubbed his hands over his face. "Shortly before Anna turned one, Mom blew his brains out with his own hunting rifle."

Holy hell.

That one stunned me. Even knowing that a prison sentence had been involved, no one could've prepared me for that.

I swallowed dryly and wondered if I should pour him some rum. Or perhaps that was in poor taste, considering the theme of the story.

"A few of us testified in her defense," he said tiredly. "She had coworkers who knew he'd been abusive too, so the lawyer managed to get it reduced to manslaughter. There was no evidence to support first-degree murder, but there was some doubt that it was strictly self-defense. Which it hadn't been. So, she went to prison."

She'd been gone six years, if I remembered correctly.

"She knew she'd been part of the problem." Peyton cleared his throat. "She begged for forgiveness for leaving me alone with Anna—but she said she had to take herself out of the equation too."

I had no words. Wanting to show him that I wasn't going anywhere, I gathered his hand in both of mine and pressed my lips to his knuckles.

I couldn't imagine what it must've felt like.

"This doesn't bother you at all?" He seemed to ask just to make sure.

"Of course it bothers me, Peyton. It bothers me that you had to go through this—all of you."

"Right, but—" He sighed and stared at me. "What would your parents think?"

I blinked.

Then I couldn't help but laugh. I kept it short and managed to contain it with a cough, but goddamn.

"Some people care about these things," he argued. "You've told me your folks are fancy as shit."

I hadn't used those words, but that was neither here nor there. "First of all," I said with a chuckle, "they dine with Kennedys, not Romneys. Second of all, even if they were dining with the Queen of England and had a list of demands for me, it wouldn't matter. They've never had that kind of hold on me." I paused. "There isn't a soul I would hide our relationship for. That said, I believe *you* will want us to stay under the radar at the office for a while. Because even if I made us exempt from the no-fraternization rule or scrapped it altogether, office gossip can get vicious, and you may want some form of a social life in Boston."

He nodded and stared at our joined hands.

He had a lot on his mind, I could tell, and I wanted him to get back on topic. He hadn't finished his story.

I pushed back a piece of his hair and brushed my thumb over his cheek. "Did your mother go to rehab before or after she'd been to prison?"

"After." He didn't look up from our hands. "It's part of the trust issues I have today. She's been to rehab twice since getting out, and she tried to hide the problems both times." He swallowed. "I'm not being entirely fair to her. The first time, she was just overwhelmed and trying to catch up. She didn't want me to lift a finger—or rather, she wanted me to focus on my own life for once, so she worked all hours of the day, pretty much."

"She handled the stress with alcohol," I guessed.

He dipped his chin. "Second time was shame. She felt like a

failure, and instead of talking to me about it—which she said would be to *burden* me—" he rolled his eyes "—she hit the bottle. And just like the first time, I found out eventually, and I shipped her off to rehab."

My God. My heart went out to him. I hadn't been in his shoes, or remotely close to being there, and even I felt a pang of betrayal and hopelessness.

"Part of me keeps waiting for the next time, you know?" He withdrew from my touch and ran a hand through his hair. "That's why it's not really fair of me. All that happened in a pretty short period of time after she got out. She's been sober for over three years now."

"Three years isn't very long when compared to everything you've been through," I reasoned.

"Maybe," he conceded. "But it's different this time. She took night classes and got a better job at the hospital. She was a nurse before—now she has a more administrative role. Less stress, higher pay, reasonable hours. She found a better apartment, she's happier, and she goes to therapy sometimes just to check in with herself. She doesn't hide anymore."

"I'm glad to hear it." I smiled carefully.

He returned it and rested his head on my shoulder.

It wasn't good enough for me, so I made room for him to get comfortable between my legs. "Come here."

He made his way over my leg and leaned back against my chest with a long sigh.

As the burning sun touched the horizon, the sea took on an almost purple color.

I kissed the top of Peyton's head.

"My mom wants to meet you," he murmured. "She'll probably treat you like a celebrity."

I snorted softly. "Has she never met any of your previous partners?"

"She met my first girlfriend when I was thirteen. Does that count?"

I chuckled against his hair and rested a hand on his chest.

"You'll have to forgive her," he muttered. "She loves Hollywood gossip and has never been around money. She's weirdly humble and knows what to value more than a monetary fortune, but she gets starstruck by fame and success."

Oh dear. "I'm sorry to disappoint, but most of that monetary fortune didn't come from me," I replied. "It's my grandfather's work."

When he died, I bought my penthouse, and I gave away half of the inheritance to my grandfather's favorite cause because he once lost his twin brother to leukemia. The rest sat untouched in various bonds, stock portfolios, and accounts, I explained to Peyton. I told him everything. It made me a bit uncomfortable to discuss it, but I figured he should know. I was one of those who'd literally been born with a silver spoon in his mouth, and no one wanted to hear one of us complain.

The grass may look greener on our side, but it was maintained by a guy from El Salvador, and the kids who ran on that lawn were raised by a woman who'd been flown in from England.

I shook my head and gazed up at the sky. I *didn't* have any complaints, but it felt entirely wrong to glorify what I'd grown up with.

"I was lucky to have my grandfather," I said. "He was down-to-earth, and he quickly taught me to build my own family. Blood wasn't everything."

Peyton tilted his face up to look at me. "That's what you did with Sandra and Mona."

I nodded and dipped down to kiss him. I kissed him unhurriedly, reconnecting after all the heavy talk, and his presence stabilized me.

"It's what I'm hoping to do with you too," I murmured. "You don't know how happy you make me, Peyton."

Breaking the kiss as little as possible, he turned around and straddled my thighs instead. Then he kissed me hard and locked his arms around my neck.

Sheer serenity flooded my senses, and I squeezed him to me.

CHAPTER 13.

"Almost," Peyton gasped.

"Shh, baby." I gnashed my teeth and gripped the counter with one hand, using the other to stroke myself off.

I clenched around his cock, intensifying the sensations with that delicious burn I craved.

He whimpered and pressed his face against my back, and he fucked me faster, losing control of his movements. He was so close. I felt it everywhere, in his breaths, in how he gripped my hips.

"Time to come, baby boy," I urged under my breath. "Daddy's close too."

I watched us in the mirror above the sink as he lost it. Head thrown back, that lethal expression of both agony and unbridled pleasure, eyes closed. He bit his lip and pumped into me a few more times, and it was about all I could take. I needed my cock shoved down his throat right fucking now.

"Oh God," he breathed, collapsing against me.

"*Kneel*," I gritted out.

He shuddered and drew out from me, then sank to his knees as I spun around on him. I grabbed his jaw and didn't waste a second. I pushed my cock between his lips and threaded my fingers into his hair. Then I pushed forward, quick thrusts, deep thrusts, hard thrusts.

He choked on me.

He left marks on my thighs with his blunt nails.

I inhaled deeply, filling my senses with the smell of us, and it pushed me right there. I tensed up and sucked in a sharp breath. Peyton redoubled his efforts, the wet sounds of the suction finishing me off. I couldn't take it. The orgasm rocketed through me.

Peyton hummed and swirled his tongue around my cock, sucking each rope of come down his throat.

"Such a good boy." I bit back a breathless groan and leaned back against the counter. "Jesus Christ. I needed that."

He went the extra mile and licked me clean before he tucked me back into my boxer briefs and zipped up my dress pants. "You've turned me into a cock addict."

My sweet boy. I cupped the back of his neck and met him in a deep kiss, our tongues mingling, our breaths slowly returning to normal. We were down to the last couple minutes. We had to leave the bathroom.

We righted each other's clothes in between kisses, and I told him to go out first.

I had to clean up the mess he'd made in me anyway.

He grinned shyly and blushed when I said that.

"I like making a mess in you, though."

I chuckled and gave him one last kiss. "So do I, love. Now, you go first."

"Yes, sir." He washed his hands quickly first, then made his way out of the bathroom.

A couple minutes later, it was my turn.

I adjusted my tie in the mirror and shrugged on my suit jacket.

After leaving the bathroom, I returned to the others in the bustling lounge, but not before getting a drink at the bar.

Peyton and Julia were raiding the snack table by the buffet.

It felt ludicrous, but I was going to miss the hell out of him. Even though it was only four days. Checking my watch as I sat down across from Cathryn and Mathis, I saw that Peyton needed to go to his gate soon. His flight for Seattle departed in an hour. The rest of us would wait an additional forty minutes for our flight to Boston.

"Daddy, we got a cookie for you," Julia said, walking toward our table.

"That's sweet of you, darling." I accepted the cookie and placed it on a napkin next to my scotch. "Want to sit with me?"

She shook her head and waited for Peyton. "Later, Daddy."

I laughed. Very well.

Once Peyton had returned and taken his seat next to mine, Julia climbed up on his lap instead.

"By the way," he said, reaching for something in his pocket, "I have something for you, sir."

I took a sip of my drink, accepting a Post-it note, and I turned it over.

I, Edward Francis Delamare, hereby pledge to call Peyton Dylan Scott twice a day until we're reunited again.

Fucking hell. The Caribbean... I could think of worse places to fall in love.

Peyton extended a pen to me too. "Just sign there at the bottom."

"Of course." I scribbled my signature and smiled as I handed the note back to him.

It was utterly juvenile and exactly what I needed now.

"Thanks." He smiled back, pleased as punch.

That evening, I stepped out of the elevator and into my home with a screaming toddler and too much luggage, and I took one sweeping glance at my place and suddenly loathed it.

What had I been thinking when I'd agreed to that dining room table?

It *was* a bachelor pad from the eighties.

"Do you miss Peyton as much as I do?" I asked.

Julia wailed and pushed at me. "I don't know!"

I sighed and set her down on the floor.

She planted her butt on the floor and smacked the floor-boards. "I don't wanna sit here, Daddy!"

Then why did she—Christ. "McDonald's for dinner?" I suggested.

It didn't stop her from sobbing her heart out, but she did nod.

"Peyton be here t-tomorrow?" she cried.

Damn it. Toddlers and the concept of time. Not the best combination. Peyton had tried to explain it before he'd left. She'd been so upset, but more than that, confused. Because "her fwriend" lived with us now. Peyton was supposed to come with us. She'd nodded uncertainly when he'd explained that they'd see each other in four sleeps. He'd counted down on her fingers.

"Almost, darling. You'll go to bed a few times, and then he'll be here." I picked her up off the floor and left the luggage behind. "Let's run you a bath, and then we'll eat McDonald's on the couch in our pajamas. How does that sound? We'll find a funny movie."

She sniffled and wiped her nose on her arm. "I want fwries, not apple slices."

"Fries, it is." I nodded firmly and opened the gate to the stairs. "And a milk shake?"

"Yeah," she whimpered.

My poor, exhausted little girl. And her poor, love-sick father.

The only thing I had going for me right now was Julia's bath bubbles that turned the entire bathtub pink. A layer of sparkly pink foam blanketed the water and managed to calm her down enough to enjoy her bath.

I sat on the toilet lid and loosened my tie, doing flight math and considering time zones. He should have landed, and it was three hours earlier...meaning he'd likely go straight to his home-town two hours north of Seattle. Or would he stay in his apart-ment and head up to his mother and sister tomorrow? Either way, I was texting him.

We're home, and we miss you already. By the way, why didn't you tell me my dining room table looks awful? I'm buying a new one. Unless you take charge, I'm thinking...gold table with furry seats.

I grinned when I saw the moving dots appear on the screen right away.

His reply popped up shortly after.

Edward!

I miss you too. Both of you.

But seriously, I don't know if you're joking about the table, given your history...

I chuckled. He'd taken the bait quickly.

So, I texted him a list of demands and gave him a budget. Only he could fix this mess. I was useless in that department, evidently. Deciding a theme for a hotel was much easier.

I finished with a mild threat.

If you don't comply, (and throw in rush deliv-ery), I will buy a gold table. Moreover, I will paint the brick walls neon green.

His attempt to sass me earned him a raised brow.

Maybe I'll deny you dickpics.

I snorted and sent Julia a quick glance. She was playing with her ponies.

Dickpics...

You'll do no such thing. I advise you to choose your next words wisely, pet.

That worked, and his response made me smile.

I'll obey, Daddy.

Good boy. You have my details, and I trust you know our address.

That "our" was on purpose. It looked good.

Two sleeps later, Julia and I found ourselves eating milk and cereal at the kitchen island while two men assembled our new dining room table.

"What do you think?" I asked Julia.

She eyed the men and the table critically. "Peyton picked it?"

I nodded.

I liked the table. It was wood—or "heavy oak," as per the description. And it fit in with the building better. It was more natural.

"Then I like it." Julia filled her mouth with Froot Loops, milk dribbling down her chin. "There are so many boxes."

Indeed. Peyton had gone nuts and ordered significantly more than I thought was possible on that budget. From textiles —throw pillows and blankets—and picture frames to new chairs and a coffee table. The hallway was filled with stacked boxes and furniture.

I supposed when you didn't order through an interior design agency, you could get more for the same amount of money.

I was spoiled at times. Clueless at others.

Peyton would have to help me with the rest. I just wanted the table and chairs in place for dinner tonight.

It took the two men about half an hour to assemble the table, and by then, Julia was on the couch in the living room watching Netflix. I tipped the gentlemen and thanked them before showing them out.

After arranging the six chairs around the table, I snapped a photo and sent the result to Peyton.

You are hereby in charge of everything that concerns furniture and what our home looks like. Hope you slept well. Miss you.

It was highly possible he was still asleep.

The older I became, the earlier I woke up in the morning. Peyton could snooze forever.

I didn't have much to do today, so after I'd tidied up in the living room and dining room area and I'd stacked the old chairs in the hallway, I called my cousin to ask what I could bring for the picnic tomorrow.

"I assume you'll get the same answer as the previous years," Trent said. "Hold on. Charlotte! Do you want Ed to bring anything?"

I trailed into the kitchen and poured myself another cup of coffee, sans hazelnut syrup. I'd put on a couple pounds in the Caribbean, and now was not the time to let myself go.

"Yeah, you're not bringing anything," Trent told me. "Unless you're bringing your new guy. He's invited, of course."

I smiled. "I appreciate that, but he's on the West Coast for the holiday," I replied. "I don't think he'll ask me to come save him on a white horse."

Trent laughed. "You never know. The magic words usually

come at night. You remember college, don't you? Charlotte made me miss all the fucking classes."

Classes, yes. Not the fucking part. I believed that was the one thing he didn't neglect when Charlotte called him from New York and said she missed him. My cousin would fly out to his car and drive all the way down to see her.

My phone vibrated, and I glanced at the screen quickly to see a message from Peyton.

"Just a second, Trent," I said.

Then I read the message.

I had my asshole waxed, which fucking hurt, and now I'm looking at the new table, and I can't stop bawling because I miss you—and because my ass hurts so goddamn much!

"What on earth?" I blurted out. It was too much to process.

"What?" Trent asked.

"I, uh..." I cleared my throat, and images flashed by in my mind. Images of Peyton getting waxed, images of him being upset. Christ. "I believe I just received the magic words."

Trent barked out a howling laugh.

Goodness, his text had actually flustered me. I was incredibly torn between worry and arousal, so I just stood there.

"I think I have to go," I said.

"Yeah, no shit." Trent was still laughing. "Let me know if you want us to take Jules."

Oh no, I couldn't possibly. She missed Peyton too much. I suspected he missed her a great deal too.

A moment later, I wrapped up the call with my cousin and took a deep breath.

Go to him.

"Julia!" I called. "Let's pack our bags—we're going to Seattle!"

When timing was everything, I gave Mathis free rein to get me where I needed to be, and he orchestrated our East Coast departure like the professional he was. The flights out of Boston required too many transfers or didn't depart soon enough, so he managed to get a private jet for Julia and me to take us to New York, where we ran straight through security, paused quickly to buy something for Peyton's family, then bolted to the gate for a four-o'clock takeoff.

We were the last to board the plane, and as soon as we made it to our seats in business, we collapsed in laughter—mine a lot more breathless than hers.

"You runned so fast, Daddy," she giggled.

"Daddy's a little out of shape," I admitted. Jesus Christ. I swallowed dryly and buckled us in, then shrugged out of my suit jacket and helped her take off her shoes and windbreaker. "I wonder how many things we forgot to pack."

It didn't matter. We had clothes for two days, and whatever else we needed, we could buy.

Her toothbrush.

Yep, I'd forgotten to pack her toothbrush. Oh, whatever.

As soon as we were in the air, I gained access to the Wi-Fi and had probably never been so grateful for Mathis. He'd texted me to say he'd arranged for a car to pick us up at the airport in Seattle, and it would take us straight to Peyton's hometown.

With the time difference, we should be in the small town of Camassia Cove around nine PM.

Julia crawled up in my lap and hauled out the screen from the armrest pocket, and I sent Peyton another text. He hadn't responded to my previous ones when I'd tried to check in with him.

Thinking about you, love. I was serious about the aloe cooling gel. It helps.

"You're cuddlier lately." I kissed the top of Julia's head.

"You're a good pillow." She patted my stomach.

I widened my eyes at her, not that she noticed. "Young lady, I've gained two pounds, not two tons."

"Okay," she laughed and shrugged.

What a fucking brat. I cleared my throat and shifted in my seat. Clearly, I was starting a new exercise regimen when we got home again.

There was no need to help her choose a movie. She'd become well-traveled and knew how to work any tablet, screen, and laptop to find the apps with streaming services.

She'd calmed down a lot too, and I was beginning to wonder if it was only her. I was happier and not as tired anymore. She picked up on that, surely.

"What is it that you and Peyton whisper to each other sometimes?" I asked.

It hadn't been a one-time thing by the pool in Nassau. They'd done it at the airport in Miami too, and yesterday when they were on the phone, Julia had lowered her voice to a whisper.

"It's a secret," she replied, pushing the icon for *The LEGO Movie*. "He say he miss me, I say really, and he go like this—" she nodded "—and I say me too cuz I miss him too when he's gone. It's our secret, and it's okay because best fwriends have secrets."

"My sweet child." I hugged her to me, overwhelmed by the love I felt. "One day, I'm going to teach you the concept of secrecy, but not today."

"Okay, but quiet now, Daddy." She wrestled her headphones out of her backpack and put them on.

Yeah, quiet now, Daddy.

Sorry, I fell asleep in the tub.

My ass still hurts, Daddy.

Give Julia a big hug from me.

This is insane. Two months ago, we didn't even know each other.

Can you call me?

I'd fallen asleep too, though in my seat. Now, my neck was killing me. Thank God Peyton wasn't here. He'd say something smug and snarky about his neck pillow.

"Darling." I pocketed my phone and brushed back Julia's hair. She'd passed out on my lap at some point. "Julia? We're landing soon."

Peyton had sent the last text an hour ago. He'd have to wait one more hour. I estimated we'd be in the car heading north by then.

Julia whined and stretched out, accidentally knocking her fist to my face, and I flinched and lowered the lethal weapon.

"You're going to be impossible to get to bed later," I muttered and scrubbed my hands over my face. Hell, I'd struggle to sleep tonight too.

"*You're* impossible," she yawned. "Wha's impossible?"

"Something you can't do. It's so difficult that it becomes impossible—you just can't do it." I helped her into her own seat and felt every part of my body protest when I twisted my torso.

"Impossible," she mumbled to herself with a nod. "I'm impossible not to love McDonald's."

I laughed softly and cupped her cheeks. "Do you know how much I love you?"

"Impossible!"

I smirked and gave her a smooch. "That's certainly true. You can't possibly know how much."

"Impossiblebly," she giggled. "I love Peyton."

"Join the club." I tightened her seat belt, then stowed away our tables. "Do you love Daddy too?"

She nodded. "When you don't yell at me, I love you dis much." She stretched out her arms and grunted to show how much.

"That's a whole lot. Good thing I almost never yell at you."

"You yell sometimes." She gave me this look that said, "Come on, old man. You gotta admit it."

I shook my head in amusement.

CHAPTER

14.

A man with my name on a board waited at baggage claim, and he seemed surprised by the lack of luggage, particularly since I was traveling with Julia. I only had my rollaboard carry-on, and Julia's booster seat was attached to it.

"Coming home, sir?" he asked.

His question threw me. Because suddenly, I had this image in my head of spending more time on the West Coast, and Peyton's family would be the reason. His contract at this point was sort of moot; I hoped he'd be with me as my assistant without an expiration date until he was ready to work as a teacher. But a year or forty years didn't matter. His mother and sister still lived out here, and he hadn't indicated he would be ready to move to Boston permanently.

"A second home, perhaps," I replied distractedly.

We'd have to come up with a solution, of course. I didn't want to take Peyton away from Washington if he loved it here, but maybe we could compromise. My cousin had a summer residence in Italy. We could have one here.

"I'm hungry," Julia complained.

"I know, darling. We'll get something to eat." I buckled her into her seat in the car and closed the door. As soon as the driver joined us, I said, "A quick stop at the nearest McDonald's drive-thru before we leave the city, please."

"Yes, sir."

We had to lay off the McDonald's. Soon.

Once we pulled away from the curb, I brought out my phone and called Peyton.

"Are you calling Peyton?" Julia demanded.

"Yes—"

"Hey!" Peyton picked up. "I was gonna text you again, but I didn't wanna come off like a needy fucking child."

I laughed, so relieved to hear his voice again. "I like it when you're needy, love."

"Hi, Peyton!" Julia shouted.

I winced at the volume.

"Oh, she's up late. Tell her I said hi. I miss her so much," Peyton sighed. "And you. Fuck. This is harder than I thought it would be."

"He says he misses you very much," I told Julia, covering the phone a bit.

She nodded, satisfied.

"Well, I officially throw in the towel," I announced. "You're in your hometown, I assume?"

"Yeah. There's some community picnic in the park tomorrow that we'll go to, I think. Mom's picking up some extra shifts at the hospital, so she's on call."

"Sounds nice. Should Julia and I bring anything?"

Peyton chuckled. "Huh?"

I smiled. "Give me your mother's address, baby. Julia and I just landed in Seattle."

There was a beat of silence before Peyton's quiet voice filtered through again. "Please tell me you're not joking, Edward."

"You're not joking, Edward," I said.

Julia gave me a strange look, and I mentally high-fived myself for the excellence in my delivery of a dad-joke.

"Holy shit," Peyton exclaimed unsteadily. "You're really on your way?"

My mirth faded when I heard the uncertainty in his tone. "We'll be there in two hours, love. I promise. I just need the address."

He swallowed audibly. "Okay. Okay. Shit, I can't believe you. Oh my God, I'm gonna see you both tonight. I'll text you the address—fuck, I gotta tell Mom. She'll go ballistic if I don't give her a heads-up. Address, right—texting you right now." Without another word, he hung up.

I grinned to myself.

It was too dark to get much of an impression of Peyton's hometown, but from what little I saw, it definitely had potential. We drove through patches of forest and a cobblestone neighborhood called Cedar Valley. Signs for places such as Silver Beach, Olympic Falls, and Downtown Marina with the ferry to the Chinook Islands made it abundantly clear that we were a long way from Boston.

This seemed like a place where I could go fishing again.

We arrived in what I assumed was a working-class neighborhood, although back home, these three- and four-story buildings would fit right in. Peyton had once told me he'd grown up in the "bad part of town," but I supposed it depended on what you compared it with.

After passing an empty square, the driver made a couple turns before he announced we were here.

I peered out of my window just as the hall inside the building lit up. A second later, Peyton appeared in the window and opened the door. He smiled widely and jogged down the steps.

"Theu's Peyton!" Julia exclaimed. She was out of her booster seat in a flash, and then she was climbing over my lap to get out first.

I grinned and let her out before I followed.

"Hi!" She ran straight into him, and he picked her up and hugged her tightly.

"Holy fuck, have I missed you, sweetheart."

I joined the two on the curb and gave Peyton a hard kiss. "It turns out we're nothing but a couple miserable McDonald's regulars without you."

He exhaled a laugh and fidgeted with my tie. "So, don't let me leave again. I don't know what I was thinking."

"We'll learn from our lesson." I gave him one more kiss before I dealt with the driver. Peyton and Julia could catch up for a while; soon, he'd be mine.

"Have a good Fourth of July, sir," the driver said and shook my hand.

"Likewise." I tipped him, then strapped the booster seat to my rollaboard.

Julia was going a mile a minute about how fast Daddy had run in New York so we wouldn't miss the flight, and Peyton was soaking it all up with a big smile.

"Darling, we have all night to talk about how fast Daddy can run," I reminded her. "Tell Peyton why we were running in the first place."

She furrowed her brow and hooked an arm around Peyton's neck. "We were in a hurry."

I chuckled and bent down to open the outside pocket of my carry-on. "Partly because we couldn't decide on the gifts for Peyton's mother and sister."

"Oh Christ, honey, you didn't have to get them anything," Peyton said in a rush.

"Nonsense. It's the first time we meet your family. It's customary to bring something." I handed the two folded-up bags to Julia, who'd already declared that she wanted to give the gifts to them. "You'll have to forgive my lack of creativity. We were in a rush, and, well, I don't know your family yet."

Julia scratched her nose and flung the two bags over her shoulder. "I wanted to pick a Minion lunchbox, but Daddy say no. It had chocolate in it!"

"And that right there was why I asked the saleslady for assistance," I finished.

Peyton laughed softly and pressed a kiss to Julia's cheek. "You're amazing—both of you. And my mom is probably pacing in the hallway right now, so let's get this show on the road."

"Want me to carry Jul—"

"Hell no. You had your turn." Peyton turned on his heel and walked up the steps.

"I can walk," Julia said casually.

"Not now." Peyton kissed the side of her head and opened the door.

I followed them, happy and amused, and we crammed ourselves into a tiny elevator to take us to the third floor.

Peyton watched me with so much affection in his eyes that it was almost impossible not to steal him away. I needed a proper reunion. It didn't have to be anything remotely dirty, but I craved the intimacy. The long hugs, the unhurried kisses, just having him in my arms.

"You'll have to let me know if I should make reservations for the night somewhere," I mentioned.

Peyton shook his head. "Mom's gonna insist you stay. I have a room here, and we have an airbed in the closet for when Anna has friends over."

Then there would be no problems whatsoever.

As the elevator stopped, I had to admit I became nervous. I hadn't met a partner's parents in...oh, fifteen years? I hadn't dated in the traditional sense in ages.

I stepped out first and made room for Peyton to pass.

There was no time for him to open the door, though. It was ripped open from the inside, by whom I assumed was Peyton's mother. She was a short, slender woman in her midfifties, and something told me she hadn't looked like that before I'd told Peyton I was on my way. Now she wore a summer dress, had her hair up, and she'd done her makeup.

She had the same dark hair and green eyes as her son.

As if on cue, Julia became ridiculously shy and buried her face against Peyton's neck.

"Mom, this is Julia, the only girl for me."

"Hi, Julia. Aren't you adorable?" Ms. Scott, or Carol, wore the definition of an "aww" face. I couldn't blame her. My daughter was the only girl for me too. "I'm so happy to meet you. Peyton talks about you all the time."

I sent him a smile.

"I'm sorry, I'm blocking the way," Ms. Scott said, quickly sidestepping to let us in. "You must be Edward. My son talks about you all the time too." She surprised me by swooping in for a hug, and she had this genuine, beaming smile that kind of melted away my nerves.

"It's a pleasure to meet you, Ms. Scott. I hope you'll tell me what exactly it is Peyton says about me."

She tinkered a laugh while Peyton blushed and scowled at me.

Since I was the last one to enter, I closed the door and locked it.

"Well, let's not all stand here," Ms. Scott said. "Peyton,

show Edward and Julia to your room so they can leave their things. I've prepared coffee and cake in the living room."

I took off my shoes before I followed Peyton, past the kitchen to the right, the living room was up ahead, and down a hall. It was a nice place. I didn't know why Peyton had felt the need to warn me. There were pictures of Peyton and Anna everywhere, and go figure, he'd been cute as a teenager too. Gangly and carefree. Which led me to believe at least those photos had been taken before everything changed for him.

The first room we passed had a sign that read "Keep Out," along with Anna's name.

Music came from the room.

"This is me." Peyton opened the next door, and I was a little disappointed. I'd hoped for a journey back to his childhood. Instead, I was greeted by blue walls, a bed, a desk, and a TV. Then I remembered that they had moved in recent years, after Ms. Scott had landed a better job. "Most of my stuff is in Seattle," he explained.

I nodded and glanced around, then landed my gaze on him. "You should give up that lease."

"Should I?" His question seemed sincere.

Julia wanted down, so he helped her to her feet, and she started taking off her jacket.

"You should." I walked over to him and finally wrapped my arms around him. "I missed you, baby boy." I breathed him in and left a trail of kisses along his shoulder. "You belong with me. With us."

He reached up on his toes and threw his arms around my neck. "I'm so fucking in love with you."

Fucking hell.

My heart constricted, and I tightened my hold on him. "Good," I whispered and kissed him. "That makes two of us."

"Yeah?" He gave me that shy smile of his.

I kissed it. "I've never been so sure."

He sighed contentedly and sank into my embrace, exactly where I wanted him. His arms dropped to my middle, and I cupped the back of his head and kissed his hair. With a glance over my shoulder, I saw that Julia was inspecting a stack of books on the desk. Considering they all had titles related to the Civil War, I doubted she'd find them interesting.

"Let's go have coffee with your mother," I murmured against the top of Peyton's head. "Then I'm gonna hold you all night." Sliding my nose down to his neck, I dropped kisses along the way and whispered in his ear, "I'll need a quick look at your bottom too."

He shuddered and nodded. "Yes, sir."

"Milk or sugar, Edward?"

"No, that's good, thank you." I shifted in my seat on the couch and took a sip of my coffee. Despite that I craved alone time with Peyton, I was more relaxed now and could enjoy myself. And I had Peyton next to me, with Julia climbing on us like a monkey. Right now, she was wildly curious about the treats on the plate Ms. Scott had prepared. It looked like chocolate cake with an assortment of cookies scattered around it.

"Julia." I got her attention and nodded at the plastic bags on the floor under the coffee table. "Did you want to give them to Ms. Scott?"

"Oh, it's Carol, please." Carol turned toward the hallway. "Anna! Come say hi, at least!" She sent me an apologetic smile. "She's off to summer camp in a couple days and has packed and repacked her bag all week."

"Summer camp—sounds exciting." I folded one leg over the

other and draped an arm along the back of the couch. It gave me free access to rub Peyton's neck. "Is it local?"

"Chinook Islands," Peyton said with a nod. "You can see them from the marina—Mom, quit it."

What had I missed?

"What?" Carol was confused too, albeit more defensive. "You're so cute together. Excuse me for being happy."

Ah. I kept my smirk to myself and watched Julia instead. She'd collected the two bags and was on her way around the table to reach the chair where Carol sat.

"But you're staring," Peyton argued.

"Should I look at the wall instead?" Carol lifted a brow.

I chuckled silently and gave Peyton's neck a squeeze. "Relax, love," I said quietly.

Peyton huffed and leaned back a bit more. His hand on my leg was anything but relaxed.

"Dis for you, and dis for Peyton's sister." Julia extended the two bags to Carol.

I took the opportunity to press a kiss to Peyton's temple and murmur for only him to hear. "What's got you worked up? Things are going well."

He took a breath and let it out slowly. "You're right. I don't know why I'm nervous."

Julia's shyness hadn't disappeared completely, so she darted back to me as soon as Carol started gushing about the presents. She said over and over that we shouldn't have bought them anything, and I waved it off. What kind of heathen arrived empty-handed when they wanted to impress a partner's parents?

Impress wasn't the right term, but I wasn't above collecting brownie points.

Anna showed up around the time Carol was fawning over

her new pashmina scarf that the saleslady insisted worked well in the summer too, especially in a state like Washington.

"Feel how soft it is, hon." She extended the scarf to Peyton. "Feel it."

He humored her. "Yeah, it's soft." He cleared his throat and addressed Anna next. She'd inherited her mother's pretty looks, but she was definitely a tomboy. *Thank fuck I hadn't let the saleslady pick a gift set of makeup.* "Anna, this is Edward and Julia."

"Nice to meet you, Anna," I said with a polite smile. "I've heard a lot about you."

"I bet we've heard more about you." She twisted her lips into a smirk that she directed at Peyton.

"You can fucking shush," Peyton told her.

I grinned. *This was going to be a good stay.*

Anna ignored her brother and sat down on the armrest of Carol's chair, rather than taking the empty chair on the other short end of the table. "Let me see?" She touched the scarf gingerly, and Carol told her there was a gift bag for her also.

"Oh." Anna blushed. *Just like her brother.*

Julia perched herself on my lap, observing the Scotts, and played absently with the hair on the back of my neck.

Anna lifted the lid to her box, and I was relieved to see her surprised but honest smile. "Oh, wow. Thank you. This is so cool."

"What is it?" Peyton leaned forward a little, and Anna held up the leather-bound journal.

He'd told me once she was an avid writer, which had been the only helpful thing I'd had to offer the saleslady.

"It's beautiful. You have to bring it to camp, sweetie." Carol touched the tie around the journal.

"Yeah." Anna stood up and clutched the journal. "I'm gonna go pack it. Thank you again, Edward."

"You're very welcome, dear." I inclined my head.

Okay, maybe I could actually pull this off.

Julia fell asleep earlier than I thought she would, considering she'd slept on the plane. Then again, it was three hours later on the East Coast, and it'd been an eventful day.

Either way, there were no complaints from me. While she slept peacefully on the airbed at the foot of Peyton's bed, I got to cuddle the hell out of my boy.

"Part of me still can't believe you're here." He burrowed deeper into my arms and kissed my chest. "That you came all this way. For me."

I hummed and reached over him to grab the bottle of cooling gel on his nightstand. "It wasn't just you. I felt I hadn't collected enough miles these past few months."

He chuckled drowsily.

"Lie flat on your back," I ordered softly.

He drew a breath, the air between us changing slightly, and obeyed me. I loved how the shift came so suddenly, how the tension could crackle with just a few words.

"If we're really quiet..." He trailed off with a pleading tone.

"No funny business tonight." I coated two fingers with gel before placing the bottle on the other side of him. "Spread your legs for Daddy." I waited until he'd complied, then eased my hand between his legs. "I do think we should check out the housing market here, though. It would be nice to have a place of our own for when we visit."

"Are—shit." He gasped when I slid my two wet fingers straight over the smoothest little hole ever. "Are you kidding me?"

"God," I muttered. "You're gonna make me hard in two

seconds, baby. You feel so soft and smooth." I could tell he was extra sensitive, both in the good way and the bad. "No, I'm not joking," I added as an afterthought. "I want you in Boston with me, Peyton. I want us to build a life there—without leaving the one you've made for yourself here." I went on to explain, hoping he'd understand, that I couldn't up and leave—or work so far away from headquarters for extended periods of time—but that we could arrange for West Coast summers and holidays.

Easter was the only holiday I wanted to spend in Boston, for Sandra's mother's sake. We'd established a tentative tradition of getting together so Mags could see Julia. Mags saw her own daughter in Julia, and it was painful, so I knew it would take a long time before the two would form a more significant bond. I had hopes, though. Mags had been overjoyed when Sandra had announced her pregnancy.

"So yes, I think a summer residence out here would be good," I said. "Besides, work does sometimes bring us here. Westwater has two locations in Seattle, one in Tacoma, and two in Vancouver. It makes sense."

Peyton nodded jerkily and pressed his knuckles to his mouth.

"Is something wrong?" I wondered.

He inhaled sharply, his abs clenching. "I'm trying to pay attention, but it's kinda difficult when you're fingering me."

"Ah. In my defense, it's absurd to think I'd be able to stay away." I added the second finger and curled them inside him. He slapped his hands to his face and arched his back. Such stunning reactions. "I trust that you understand you'll go back to the spa regularly from now on."

He'd never had much hair to begin with, but I couldn't resist what I was feeling now. It was a miracle I hadn't already buried my face between his legs. But I suspected the stubble on my chin would hurt him too much.

"Yes, Daddy," he whimpered under his breath.

I couldn't resist his cock either. It lay there, hard, pointing toward his abs, and my mouth watered.

"You're going to have to be quiet," I whispered. I leaned over his stomach and licked the underside of his cock. At the same time, I started massaging his prostate. "Promise Daddy."

"I p-p-promise," he stuttered in a breath. "Oh God."

I hummed around his cock and took him as far as he'd go.

EPILOGUE

YEARS LATER

"You need to relax." I steered Peyton into our bedroom and sat him down on the edge of the bed. "You were supposed to take it easy this summer, not take on extra projects."

I was incredibly happy for him; his podcast had taken off since it'd been recommended in not one but two history-themed magazines. But since he'd also taken on one gig as a substitute teacher in Boston and one out here in Camassia as a teacher in summer school, he wasn't getting the rest he needed. Hell, at times, he worked more than I did.

"I was almost done," he defended petulantly. "And preparing for an interview isn't an extra project. It's part of the job. I've never interviewed an author for an episode before." He huffed as I got down on one knee and removed his socks. "For the record, I would've finished hours ago if I didn't have to go through Livie's notes on your presentation. Does she honestly call that proofing?"

I kept my amusement to myself and unbuttoned his pants. I feared he was stricter toward my office assistant than I was. Peyton refused to let go, for which I was secretly pleased, but Livie was the second-best assistant I'd ever had.

Peyton still worked for me, though he'd cut his hours in order to juggle our rather busy life. He handled everything concerning business trips and bigger projects; Livie was "stationed" outside of my office in her own cubicle. In short, Peyton had become a coordinator and sometimes a bossy little fucker. He knew my schedule better than I did and came and went at headquarters as he pleased.

"You should cut her some slack," I advised. "She's doing fine."

"Oh, is she?" Peyton cocked a brow. "Did you know that she booked you in for Milan in September initially?"

I furrowed my brow and tugged down his pants. "I thought Milan was in August."

The ratings for our East Coast locations had finally picked up, and now we were planning on rebranding some of our European hotels too. We were targeting two of our most popular lines, including the one geared toward business travelers, which we had renamed with a heavy marketing campaign. Lately, much to my joy, it had become a *thing* for younger travelers to let people know they were staying at a Westwater Vision hotel.

There were popular hashtags involved. Serious business.

It was what it had boiled down to. We'd needed to rebrand and offer a more personalized stay in order to bring back a lost demographic. Additionally, thanks to our exchange program between our locations in New York and Los Angeles, we'd discovered that our LA staff was generally better at adjusting their approach depending on the clientele. A seasoned businessman who worked in finance spoke a language different from, say, a younger woman who flew in from Silicon Valley for a tech-related seminar. Something our East Coast employees were more aware of now.

Peyton lifted a bit so I could pull down his briefs too. "It's in August *now*. Because I intervened. I told her *again* that Julia and I wouldn't be able to go with you once school starts, and then I changed it."

"Ah." I smirked faintly as I unbuttoned his shirt. "You're adorable when you get demanding and huffy, but you can lay off the attitude now."

It served as a reminder to take him down a peg or two, which I had no issue doing. He thrived on having a lot to do, and he loved organizing and coordinating, but he spiraled if he didn't get his mental downtime. Time to let go of everything, time to lower his defenses, time to let Daddy take over.

"I'm not giving you attitude." Peyton frowned. "I'm just saying—"

"*Quiet*," I commanded with a hitched brow in warning.

He snapped his mouth shut.

Better.

I removed the rest of his clothes in comfortable silence, then guided him into the bathroom.

"We have the house to ourselves. Let's enjoy it." I turned on the water and waited for it to get warm.

We needed this. Most days, he was the wonderful man who'd become the love of my life. A man whose personal journey I was lucky to be part of. A terrific father to Julia. Far better in the kitchen than I was. He'd turned our Boston home into a place I couldn't wait to get back to at the end of the day. A man who dressed sharply for work, a man who threw off the suit and changed into sweatpants as soon as he got home, a man of intelligence and heart. But between him and me... When it was just the two of us, he would forever be my little boy.

I took my time washing him under the hot spray, hoping I washed away more than the day. For one night, it was only us. "Forget everything else." I massaged the shampoo into his hair and felt the tension rolling off him. "Julia's probably forgotten us by now."

Peyton smiled quickly.

Over the years, his sister had become Julia's role model.

When Anna was home from school in Seattle, Julia demanded to go see Nana and Aunt Anna. She made them visit us in Boston often too, not afraid to show her puppy-dog eyes over FaceTime. Julia'd even convinced both Anna and Carol to visit for her first day of school this fall.

"Did I mention I got new advertisers on the podcast?" Peyton asked.

"You did, and that's not what I call forgetting everything else." I dipped down and kissed him chastely. "Don't make me regret turning our study into a recording studio, pet."

He grinned impishly. "I don't think a studio mic and some software qualify as—"

"Hey." I tugged his hair harder, hard enough for him to wince and take the hint.

"Ow," he whispered. "Sorry."

"It's okay, baby. I know you're excited." I eased up and grabbed the showerhead. "I'm very proud of you."

That seemed to do the trick. He sighed contentedly, and he tilted his head back as I washed away the shampoo.

After securing the showerhead in the mount again, I poured body wash into my hand and started rubbing the kinks out of his shoulders. Down his back, over his chest, between his ass cheeks...

He shivered and hummed. "You know when I need a break."

"It's one of the best responsibilities a Daddy can have." A role that had become part of my identity with Peyton. "I love taking care of you."

He smiled serenely. "I love pleasing you."

I kissed him softly and soaped up his cock properly. "You always do."

He proved it every time he tried to insert himself into tasks at work that weren't his to perform anymore. He demanded perfection for me, down to the coffee I was served and how I received my briefings in the morning. "It has to be done *right*, Daddy," he'd complain sometimes. He'd become genuinely distraught when unexpected events threw off my schedule, which happened to everyone. But he hated it with a passion.

Once we were both showered and clean, I turned off the water and patted him dry with a towel.

He regressed further when I reached a ticklish spot, and he let out a giggle.

"There's my sweet boy." It was an addictive sight that never failed to flood my senses with possessiveness and lewd ideas. "Go sit on the bed. I'm going to grab a toy for us."

"Yes, sir!" He tightened the towel around his hips and left the bathroom.

I took a calming breath and squatted down to open the cupboard underneath the sink. It was where we kept our toy box, and I was in the mood for a prostate massage tonight.

I folded the bean-shaped egg and a bottle of coconut oil into a towel and joined Peyton in the bedroom.

He flushed when he spotted me. "You're always naked, Daddy."

"Daddy likes to be naked with his boy." I set the towel aside for now and got down on one knee between his legs again, a position I'd thought about more and more lately. While Peyton had already started planning my fiftieth birthday celebration next year, I was growing antsy for him to have my name when the day came. We'd already discussed him adopting Julia, although more from a practical point of view. If anything happened to me, there was only one person good enough to raise our girl, and it was Peyton.

Parting his towel, I placed a kiss on the inside of his thigh.

"Oh," he exhaled. He covered his semi-hard cock with his hands, and I trailed inward to get a proper taste. He made a needy little noise when I sucked one of his smooth balls into my mouth. "Ohh, I like that so much."

"Mmm..." So did I. I tongued and sucked on his balls until he was rock hard behind his hands. Then I removed his hands and put him in my mouth.

His thighs trembled with how he tensed up, and he shifted his hands into my hair. "Do you like my cock a lot, Daddy?"

I shook my head and sucked him harder on the upstroke, then kissed the wet tip. "I love it. I'm gonna suck the come from it after I've filled your tight little bottom."

"Oh," he whined. "I wanna do that right now, please. It's been *forever*."

I smirked and rose to my feet, making it look a lot more graceful than it felt. "It's been two days, dear."

"That's forever," he sang.

I chuckled and crawled over to the middle of the bed. "Come here, then. Let's cuddle our special way."

"*Yesss*." He snuggled up in my arms and didn't waste any time. As I brushed my fingers along his back, he leaned over my chest and closed his mouth around one of my nipples. His hand that wasn't trapped between us went to my cock. He liked tugging on it and playing with it when it was soft—and sometimes pouted when it turned hard. Until he realized he liked that even more.

He was such a precious, expressive boy.

Desire zinged and zapped from my chest down to my cock.

He lifted his head after a while and frowned at me. "You're getting hard too fast. I thought getting older would take care of that."

I stifled a laugh. "I'm very sorry that you turn me on to this extent. I'll work on it."

He huffed. "I'm just saying. It's okay for boys to come in two minutes, not for Daddies."

"Oh, is that a fact?" I rumbled a chuckle, finding him too cute for words. "When was the last time I came in two minutes?"

"I dunno. Never? But you get my point."

"I'm not sure anyone would, pet. Getting hard and coming are two very different things. I thought you knew that." I pointed to my cock. "Now, put that mouth of yours to better use and show Daddy your sweet little hole."

It was the one position that still flustered him, even to this day. It was part of why I loved it. My blushing boy with his ass in my face—life didn't get much better than that.

Before he could turn around and hitch a leg over me, I grabbed the oil and stuffed an extra pillow behind my head. Then he straddled my face and scooted forward slightly.

"That's perfect," I murmured. "Suck me, beautiful."

He nuzzled the base of my cock and snaked his tongue around me, slowly coating me with saliva before he reached the head and engulfed me in wet warmth.

I released a breath and drizzled some oil between his ass cheeks.

It was an intoxicating sight, seeing how the glistening oil trickled over his soft, smooth ass.

"Don't come all over my chest this time." I ghosted two fingers over his opening and spread the coconutty liquid.

"It happened *once*," he defended.

"Because you've turned into an ass-slut, just like your Daddy." I kept rubbing the oil into his sensitive flesh, my digits gliding with ease. "You didn't even touch yourself. You just fucked yourself on my fingers like a desperate little whore, and then you were spraying your come in Daddy's chest hair."

He whimpered and clenched around the tip of my finger. "I couldn't help it," he implored.

I responded by hooking my arms under his thighs and

pulling him back to my face. Then I tongued his asshole, kissed it deeply, and grazed my teeth over the soft protrusions.

Peyton gasped, only to exhale a long, pleading moan.

I managed to reach his neck, a silent command to lower himself over my cock again.

"Good boy," I murmured huskily. I set an unhurried pace, undulating my hips to slide the head of my cock against the back of his throat. "Fuck my tongue, Peyton. I know you want to."

He found that embarrassing, much to my delight. He constantly needed that shove before he tumbled into a pool of his own depravity. Nothing turned me on more than providing the push.

"Don't be shy, little one. You love it when I fuck myself on your tongue too, don't you?"

"That's different," he mewled, stroking me off. "Oh God…" He sank into my touch when I replaced my tongue with my fingers instead. "I need your cock, Daddy. It feels so good. I miss it. Daddy, I miss it."

His words went straight to my cock, and I had to suppress a groan.

Making him desperate always worked. Once he was fucking my fingers with his urgent moans following each thrust, I returned to using my tongue instead, and he was past shame and boundaries. He just plain needed.

It was then I could switch things up. It was then I had him where I wanted.

Ordering him to insert a toy into my ass, I helped him off me and repositioned the pillows behind me so I could half sit. At this point, he'd do anything I said.

"Can I kiss you down there first, please?" he asked.

"Another time," I promised. "I want you riding my cock within the next minute. Daddy's gonna watch you."

"Oh." He grinned nervously and coated the egg in oil, carefully avoiding the string at the end. "I better make it good for you, then." When he slid the curved toy between my cheeks, I sucked in a breath and exhaled slowly, pushing back until it was all in.

Oh, fucking hell, that's it.

"Highest setting?" he wondered.

I nodded quickly and grabbed the oil from him. "I want your back to me."

"Yes, sir."

I moaned as the vibrations sent a rush of pleasure through me, and I slicked up my cock hurriedly, coating myself with oil and jerking off into my fist.

"It's my turn now," he protested.

"Okay, come sit on me." I wiped my hands on the towel and helped him straddle my lap. Gripping the root of my cock, I held it so he could more easily take me inside him. And he did it so slowly, so perfectly. "That's so sexy, baby boy. The way you pull me in..." The head of my cock slipped inside and made him whimper and clench down on me. Then inch by inch, between shaky breaths and a lot of determination to please me, he took all of me.

Perfection. Every fucking time.

For several moments, all I heard was our breathing.

"This is the best feeling in the world," he whispered shallowly.

I stroked his hips and sides, kneading his flesh firmly as if I could somehow translate the powerful love I felt into a touch.

When he started moving, everything intensified. He planted his hands on my legs and rolled his hips, and I couldn't look away for a goddamn second. From the careful and tentative thrusts in the beginning, to when his need grew and he had to have more, faster, and harder.

Every time he shifted forward to withdraw from me, he

pressed my cock downward and applied force onto the vibrator within me.

"Do you like it, Daddy?" he panted.

"Don't slow down. You're doing so well, baby." I blew out a breath and slid my thumbs inward toward his ass. "You're my perfect little one, aren't you?"

"Yes," he moaned. "Fuck, I can't get enough." As one of his hands disappeared from my leg, I knew he was stroking himself. "Will there ever be a day that we're not useless when we're away from each other?"

I chuckled, out of breath, and traced the ridges around his opening with my fingers. "I doubt it, my love. That's why we have to make sure to always be together."

"Yeah." He became quiet and slowed down just a little. But then he took me deep and quickened the pace again.

The storm surged inside me, and I leaned forward to apply more pressure on the toy. *My God.* I groaned against Peyton's back and hugged him to me. "Keep going. Christ."

He was going to make me lose it. Heat spread across my skin like wildfire, and swirls of bliss began making their way through me. My pulse thrummed faster and faster.

"Daddy?" he whimpered.

"Yeah, baby."

"Why can't we get married?"

I blinked, and I forced myself to pull away from the storm. Lips pressed against the damp skin of his back, I hauled in a stuttered breath and instinctively squeezed him to me harder.

"Who says we can't?" I barely recognized my own voice. It came out rough, like I'd had a bottle of whiskey. "I've been thinking about it a lot lately."

"Really?" The hope in his tone nearly did me in.

He'd slowed down again, though now it was something else entirely that threatened to set me off.

"Really." I kissed his back, tasting the fresh perspiration, and wrapped my fingers around his cock. Jesus, he was wet with pre-come and, as fucking always, it made me salivate. "I want nothing more than to have you as my husband."

Peyton leaned back against me and tilted his face, and reflex kicked in. I cupped his cheek and kissed him hungrily.

"I love you, Peyton."

"I love you." He gasped when I twisted my hand on the downstroke, swiping the pad of my thumb over the fluids at the head. "Daddy, may I propose right now, please?"

He was going to be the death of me.

I flicked the tip of my tongue against his, our lips just barely brushing against each other. "I don't think I'll ever be able to say no to you."

He giggled breathlessly and sucked on my bottom lip. "That bodes well for my question."

I grinned into another kiss. "Propose to me."

His gorgeous eyes lit up. "Edward, will you—"

"Yes."

"Daddy!"

I laughed, only to groan because that felt fucking amazing. "Jesus Christ, Peyton, ask me to marry you before I fill your ass."

"Gah! Okay. Okay. I'm serious." Well, he was trying. "Will you marry me?"

"*Yes.*" With a death grip on his hips, I forced him to move, to fuck himself on my cock, because I couldn't take it much longer. The emotions racing through me bordered on bizarre, but my God, had he turned me into the luckiest man on earth.

Thankfully, he felt the same desperation. After another messy, wild kiss, he grabbed my legs again and lost himself in the rhythm. He rode my cock like the perfect boy he was, moaning, pleading, worshiping us, until we were both there, and then we were coming together.

We got married here last night. Right here on our private beach in Jamaica.

It's not ours, except it is. It always will be.

In front of our friends and family, we promised to love each other, to stay true, to have and to hold...

It's the easiest vow I've ever made, Edward.

Yet, I already know today is going to be better. I saw you packing Julia's adoption papers with our breakfast basket before we returned to the beach for a morning in the sun.

You'll give me those three little words that have made me the luckiest guy on the planet over and over.

"Just sign here."

MORE FROM CARA

In Camassia Cove, everyone has a story to share:

Bennett & Kieran
Mathis

Cara freely admits she's addicted to revisiting the men and women who yammer in her head, and several of her characters cross over in other titles. If you enjoyed this book, you might like the following.

Their Boy
MMM | The Game Series, #2 | BDSM | Daddykink | Standalone

Left all alone in the world after the loss of his parents, Kit Damien feared his life was over before it had truly begun. Then he met Colt and Lucas, two Daddy Doms who changed everything. The three embark on a journey to learn about true love, growing up, the importance of sprinkles, and the rules of The Game that can make them all winners.

Out
MM | Comedy Romance | Coming Out Story | Age Difference | Standalone

I had two things on my list when I arrived in Los Angeles. One, track down Henry Bennington, the uncle and guardian of my little brother's best friend Tyler, and tell him to get his ass back to Washington—because his nephew was getting out of control. And two, figure out just how non-straight I was. Nowhere on this list did it say, "Get Tyler's uncle into bed and fall for him." Nowhere.

Power Play
MM | Daddykink Romance | Age Difference | Mental Health | Standalone

Love sucked. Correction: it sucked when you were in love with your parents' closest friend and he didn't feel the same. Madigan had always been there for me, from when I was a kid to when I got drafted by the NHL. Then I made the mistake of confessing my feelings for him... I was such a loser. My bipolar disorder was already difficult to manage as it was; add high anxiety and, most recently, as the cherry on a shit sundae, a suspension from the team. Why couldn't he see that I was perfect for him? We even had kink in common! Not that he knew that...

Check out Cara's entire collection at www.caradeewrites.com, and don't forget to sign up for her newsletter so you don't miss any new releases, updates on book signings, free outtakes, giveaways, and much more.

ABOUT CARA

I'm often awkwardly silent or, if the topic interests me, a chronic rambler. In other words, I can discuss writing forever and ever. Fiction, in particular. The love story—while a huge draw and constantly present—is secondary for me, because there's so much more to writing romance fiction than just making two (or more) people fall in love and have hot sex. There's a world to build, characters to develop, interests to create, and a topic or two to research thoroughly. Every book is a challenge for me, an opportunity to learn something new, and a puzzle to piece together. I want my characters to come to life, and the only way I know to do that is to give them substance—passions, history, goals, quirks, and strong opinions—and to let them evolve. Additionally, I want my men and women to be relatable. That means allowing room for everyday problems and, for lack of a better word, flaws. My characters will never be perfect.

Wait...this was supposed to be about me, not my writing.

I'm a writey person who loves to write. Always wanderlusting, twitterpating, kinking, and geeking. There's time for hockey and cupcakes, too. But mostly, I just love to write.

~Cara.